# FAMILY DOCTOR'S BABY

## KRISTA LAKES

ZIRCONIA PUBLISHING, INC.

Family Doctor's Baby

~

From New York Times bestselling author Krista Lakes comes a sexy standalone novel about the baddest bad boy doctor and the sweet little nurse that he falls for.

When I left my small hometown years ago, I never expected to come back. I certainly never expected that when I did, I'd be working for *him*.

He's the town's doctor. He's supposed to be a respectable member of society, a pillar for the community. He's supposed to have come a long way from the bad boy who rode a motorcycle in high school.

But he hasn't. One glance from those lustful eyes looking at me tells me that he has the same voracious appetites that he did when we were younger.

Only it's not quite the same stare. It's more urgent. It's more intense. I'm not the same nerdy girl who tutored him.

I've grown up, developed fertile curves that I know he finds irresistible.

In this small town, rumors travel fast, and the family doctor can't be seen as a player. So he does try to resist. And I do too. But with every smoldering glance and moment of sexual tension, we find our barriers breaking down.

After a stressful night of touch-and-go baby delivery, a moment of elation overcomes our inhibitions. It seems like maybe we'll need to confront those rumors sooner rather than later, especially before I begin to show the results of that night.

Can I give this doctor the family he has always desired?

Dr. Matthews leaned in and brought his lips toward mine. He paused right before our lips touched. Just for a moment, though. It was as if he were making sure that I wanted this. The universe held its breath as we both held our breath. I noticed everything from the way his aftershave lingered in the air to the water droplets in his hair. After a second that felt like eternity, he leaned in the rest of the way, firmly pressing his lips against mine.

Our fate was sealed.

A soft moan made its way up my throat as I relaxed into his kiss. I closed my eyes and let my hands drift up toward his face. His beard stubble tickled my fingertips as I dragged them over his cheeks.

It must have been the adrenaline we'd both experienced that morning. Or maybe it was that the emergency had bonded us closer than ever before. I didn't know what had gotten into either of us, but I suppose it didn't need explaining. It felt good and right and that's all I really cared about. I needed a release that only he could give me.

Jacob slowly broke our kiss and dropped his hands to the top of my hips. Then he leaned in again, passionately pressing his lips to mine. My heart began to do flip flops behind my rib cage. Within a few seconds, I felt Jacob open his mouth and gently dart his tongue out, teasing it into my mouth.

A tingling sensation coursed through my body as our tongues lightly wrestled with each others, twisting around in a sensual dance. I reveled in the sensations: his taste, his smell, the way he held his body against mine. This wasn't a dream. This was actually happening.

Jacob broke the kiss and took a step back. His cheeks were flushed and his eyes dark.

"I'm sorry. That was unprofessional."

My heart hammered in my chest and my lips ached for more of his kisses.

"I don't care," I told him. "I don't want to stop."

He looked up, his eyes bright as they met mine. Desire that matched my own shone in them and my body heated. I took the step forward to bring us back together. Slowly, I brought my hand up and wrapped it around the back of his neck.

"Are you sure you're okay with this?" he asked, his hands already coming to my hips.

"Just shut up and kiss me," I said, still smiling.

# CHAPTER 1

"*D*id you get fired from your last job?"

I did a double take as I removed the stethoscope from my ears. "Excuse me?"

"Did you get fired from your last job?" Abigail St. James repeated, impatiently holding out her arm for me to take the blood pressure cuff off. The small exam room suddenly felt constricting with the former prom queen lording herself over me yet again. It had been fifteen years since high school, yet nothing had changed.

"No, I was not fired," I replied, trying to keep my voice calm as I undid the Velcro and hung up the cuff. "In fact, my boss begged me not to go."

"Sure they did." Abigail rolled her big blue eyes. "Why are you back then?"

"I wanted to be closer to my family. So I moved back and I got a job here at the clinic," I said. "Please put your finger here so I can check your pulse."

I held out the small pulse-ox finger machine. Abigail held out her left hand with a big sparkly diamond on the ring finger and then waggled her hand. She waited for me to put the machine on for her rather than just sliding her finger into the finger spot. It was her way of showing me that she was still in charge.

"I married Aiden. You remember, the football quarterback?" Abigail made sure to flash her big sparkly ring a little bit more. "We have three kids."

"Congratulations." I checked the numbers on the pulse ox and took it off her finger. Everything was normal.

"I'm sure that my son will be the quarterback just like his dad." She looked up at me with big blue eyes and a cruel smile. "While I'm sure your kids will be sitting in the stands pigging out on nachos just like you did."

Fifteen years and she was still a total bitch picking on the shy kid. Where she had been popular, I'd been the slightly chubby, quiet kid that liked reading and science. Abigail had made it her personal mission to harass me all four years of high school. Apparently that wasn't enough for her.

*I am a professional,* I reminded myself as I considered telling her that she was the one who needed to lay off the nachos now. I was the one who had seen the scale numbers. I kept my mouth shut, though. I didn't need stoop to her level.

"I don't have any children yet. I decided to focus on my career as a nurse."

"That's too bad." Abigail shrugged. "Kids are everything. I guess you'd need a husband for that, though, huh? I don't see a ring on your finger."

Her words hit me with a punch to the gut. I wanted kids. I wanted a husband and kids and a dog and the white picket fence. I just didn't have them yet. I hadn't found the right guy and I was afraid that time was slipping away from me. But, the last person I wanted to tell that to was Queen Abigail.

"Okay. Everything looks good. The doctor will be in shortly to see you." I didn't bother to smile as I went and washed my hands.

"But seriously, Hannah, why are you back?" Abigail asked. "You were free. You could have done anything. Why are you back in Riversville, Iowa?"

"Like I said, I wanted to be close to family." I dried my hands and opened the exam room door. "I'll go let Dr. Matthews know you're ready."

"At least I like Dr. Matthews being back," she mumbled.

I hurried out of the room and then leaned against the closed door. It took me a moment to regain my composure. Fifteen years since high school and yet that girl was exactly the same. Beautiful but mean. Some people never changed.

I shook my head and headed over to my small office to finish charting her information. It struck me as odd that I had an office as a nurse, but this was a small doctor's office in a small town. I'd been here for about a month, so I had things the way I wanted them. Most days it was just me, the doctor, and Donna the receptionist in the office. It was a big difference from the downtown Chicago hospital I used to work at.

"Hannah, you have a patient waiting for you in Room Three." Donna, the front secretary popped her head into my office. She had a wide smile on her face and even though it was Monday morning, she was still as cheery as always.

"Thanks, Donna," I said, quickly finishing up my charting on Abigail. "I'll be there in just a second."

Donna disappeared and I got up from my desk. When I stepped out into the hallway, I nearly ran over Doctor Matthews coming out of Abigail's exam room.

"Oops, sorry," I said, taking a step back to let him pass.

He pushed his dark hair off of his forehead and his light blue eyes lit up with a smile. He was also returning alum from Riversville High School, but I liked him a lot more than Abigail.

"Good morning, Hannah," he said, with a warm smile. "Have a good weekend?"

Just the sound of his voice made me tingle inside and my heart flip flopped behind my rib cage. I'd had a crush on him all through high school, and despite no longer being a teenager, I still didn't know how to keep my wits around him. Yet another thing that hadn't changed in the past fifteen years. This was something I was very okay with staying the same, though.

"Yeah, it was nice," I said. "I didn't do too much. Just worked on unpacking. I had no idea how much junk I had. You?"

He chuckled. "Not much. It was a quiet weekend. I was on call and didn't have to come in once."

"I guess that's the perk of a small town. It's quiet," I said with a smile. I wished I had something more clever to say, but I was just glad I was speaking in full sentences around him.

"Looks like we've got a busy week ahead." Dr. Matthews lifted up his clipboard. "We're booked solid all day today and most of the rest of the week."

"That sounds great. You know me, I love staying busy." I found myself fidgeting as I spoke. Even though I'd known him since high school and we'd even graduated together, I was still infatuated by those blue eyes of his. They were hypnotic.

"You have a good morning," he said as he stepped toward his office at the end of the hall. He flashed me one last smile that had my insides heating and knees melting. "We'll catch up later."

I nodded and then began making my way toward Room Three. The smile was still on my face from the brief interaction with my schoolyard crush as I slid the door open and stepped inside.

There, seated on the exam table, was the young Emily Markins. She was ten years my junior and I'd babysat her before going away for college. She had already been happily married since graduating high school and now had a baby on the way.

It was strange to see her like that, with a large baby bump and glowing. I felt so old. I'd babysat her while I was in high school, and here she was pregnant. On purpose. I was proud of her, but in a way a little bit jealous, too.

"Hey, Emily," I said, shaking her hand. "It's been a while. How are things down at the hardware store?"

She shrugged and flipped her hair over her shoulder. "Same old thing. Just working at my dad's store. How's being back in town?"

"It's good," I replied. "My parents are happy I'm back."

She smiled. "I can't believe you're really back, but I'm glad you're here. It's nice to have more medical people in town. Especially with the baby on the way."

Then she gently patted her round belly. A soft smile came over her face.

"Your chart says you're at thirty-five weeks, so we're going to start doing weekly exams," I told her. "You ready to see me every week?"

"Definitely. I'm getting good at peeing in the cup," she replied dryly. "Maybe with a little more practice, I'll actually be able to get most of it in there."

I chuckled and began my work. Emily patiently answered questions as we worked through her exam. She looked like a typical pregnancy and everything was progressing as planned. She smiled wide when I pulled out the handheld Doppler from the drawer and we checked the baby's heart rate. The sound of the baby's heartbeat filled the room as we listened in on him. He was a strong little guy.

"Everything looks good," I said, jotting down a few notes onto her chart. "Your blood pressure is normal and so is your heart rate. The little guy is right on target. Dr. Matthews will be pleased. Do you have any questions for me before I go and get the doctor?"

"Am I ready for this?" Her smile trembled. "I mean, I have the nursery set up and diapers ready, but... what if I screw him up? What if I'm a terrible mother?"

I reached over and squeezed her hand. "The fact that you're worried means you won't be. And know that we all screw up. It's part of being human, but as long as you love this little guy and always try to do your best, then you'll be a great mom. I've known you since you were little and I can tell you that you're going to be fantastic."

"Thanks, Hannah." Her smile steadied a little and she took a deep breath. "How many kids do you have? You're really good at this."

I paused before speaking. Apparently, this was the question of the day for me.

"I actually don't have any kids," I said.

Her eyes widened in surprise. "Oh really? I would have thought you'd have at least two by now!"

I forced the outside of my lips into a smile. "Yeah, well, I guess I haven't met that special someone yet. Until I do, no kids for me."

Emily seemed confused and saddened by the fact that I hadn't made any children yet. I suppose her reaction wasn't too surprising, though. Emily's life path was the norm for people in our small town. Everyone met their sweetheart in high school, got married and were pregnant by their early twenties. I was most definitely the odd one in town and the older I got, the more apparent that fact became.

I was already well over thirty-years-old and still hadn't met a man that I deemed worthy enough for marriage. Sure, I'd dated a bit, and even gotten close a couple of times, but it never felt right. Sometimes I felt like I was just too late to the game.

The thought of never meeting the right man or being able to have kids made me cringe, but I was a realist. I knew it was a definitely possibility that I'd grow old and have nothing and nobody to keep me company, except maybe a cat or two. I constantly worried that the ship had sailed for me and I would end up stuck on the shore, by myself, with no children to raise.

"Thanks again, Hannah," Emily said, bringing my attention to her once again.

"You're very welcome," I said. "It's good to see you again. I'll have to stop by the hardware store one of these days and say hello."

"I'd like that very much," she replied.

I left the room and closed the door behind me. Coming back home, I had expected some people to ask me questions about my life. It was only natural. Not many girls left our town, and even fewer left because they dreamed of something more. Hardly anyone came back without a good reason. I was different than what people in this town expected.

Still, the fact that every patient so far today had reminded me that I was not married and childless was enough to drive me crazy. I could only hope that the longer I was here, the less people would ask me. They would hear through the grapevine that Frank and Marla's daughter was a spinster. There would be rumors that I was gay or that I had some sad disease.

As long as the questions stopped, I would be okay with that. I'd come home for a reason and it wasn't for the town to ask me why I didn't have kids yet. I only planned on being here for a year or two. Then I'd go back to the city and my regular life.

I sat down at my desk and finished charting my notes on Emily, but my thoughts were everywhere else. They focused mostly on my dad and how he would never get to see a grandchild.

He was the reason I was back in Riversville. He was sick. Lung cancer. We'd already tried everything without success. The doctors gave him a year, and he wanted to spend it where he had spent the rest of his life. I'd moved home to be closer to him as long as I could, and to provide care once things got bad. No one in town knew how bad it was yet, and my dad wanted to keep it that way, so I was just telling everyone I was home because I wanted to be.

In reality, I was home to help my father die.

"You okay?" Dr. Matthews asked, suddenly standing in my doorway.

I startled and realized I must have looked about ready to cry.

"Yeah, I'm fine. Just thinking," I replied, doing my best to smile and look like everything was normal.

"Must have been some dark thoughts," he said. He leaned nonchalantly against the door frame, all lean lines and strong edges.

I shrugged, not wanting to bring him into my depressing world. "What can I do for you?"

"Just wanted to quickly check in with you about Emily," he said, stepping into my office.

He looked so damn handsome in his gray slacks and white button-down shirt. It made him look so professional and put together and sexy. I tried not to stare blatantly at him, but it was a battle I was loosing. Those light blue eyes of his could have made me melt in the middle of a snow storm. They always drew me in and for some reason that I couldn't explain, they always felt safe.

"She looks great. Everything with her and the baby looks normal," I replied. I rattled off the numbers I'd put in the chart.

Dr. Matthews nodded as he listened. "Okay, great. I'll let you get on with your day. Just wanted to touch base before I saw Emily."

"Sure thing," I said, with a soft chuckle. "It's no problem."

He cocked his head to the side. "You sure everything's okay, Hannah?"

"Yeah, of course." I managed a real smile this time. It was easy when he was around.

"It just seems like you've got something on your mind," he said, crossing his arms and waiting for me to bare all my secrets. I was half tempted. I wanted to bare things to him.

I shrugged. "It's still early. Maybe I need more coffee."

"Coffee can never hurt," he said with a smile.

"Yeah, you're right about that." I reached for my cup and took a sip. It was lukewarm but still better than nothing. My coffee could hold my secrets for now.

"Okay." He flashed me a quick smile and walked away. I'd be lying if I said I didn't watch him for a little longer than someone should realistically watch their boss.

I sighed and focused my attention back to my computer. I had work to do and me sitting there moping about things wasn't going to get it done. Moping wouldn't fix things, but working would at least accomplish something.

"Hannah, room two is here," Donna called to me.

Time to get back to work.

# CHAPTER 2

When the work week was over and Saturday finally rolled around, I decided to wake up a little early. Even though it was my day off, I still had a lot of things to do. My parents, who lived on the other side of town from me, were having a BBQ. It was always a huge event and it only seemed to grow every year. Half the town would end up making an appearance. Some I'm pretty sure only came for the free food, but others were genuinely interested in keeping in touch with my parents.

My dad was an active member of the town's Gentleman's Poker Society and my mother went to every Ladies' Bridge Club meeting. The poker games were real, but the bridge games were just a means to gossip and plan out the lives of everyone else in the town. All the important people in town were members, which meant that despite having a strange daughter, my parents were pillars of the community and that everyone knew who they were.

The thought crossed my mind that this might be my dad's last BBQ and my ribs tightened around my heart. I shook my head, trying not to be negative. If this was his last BBQ, I was going to make sure it was a good one and not bring gloomy thoughts with me.

I rolled out of bed and looked out my window at the morning sunshine. The view that sprawled in front of me was like something out of a farmer's magazine. My house was on the outside of town, which meant that my backyard consisted of nothing but miles and miles of corn fields. I found it beautiful and incredibly peaceful, especially in the early summer, when the corn stalks were still dark green. It looked like an ocean of lush foliage against a bright blue sky, laid out in front of me as far as the eye could see.

In the distance, a lonely red tractor puttered across my view. The sound of the motor combined with the sweet smell of summer grass triggered childhood memories. I opened the window and drew in a long breath, sucking up the humid air.

*There are things I love about this place,* I thought. *It's worth it to be back here.*

Shutting the window, I wrapped myself in my robe and went downstairs to start a pot of coffee. While it heated up, I glanced around my little house. Fifty years ago, it had been my grandparent's farm house. When my grandparents passed years ago, they'd left it to my parents and they'd used it as a second home for guests. When we got my dad's diagnosis, they were happy to give it to me so I could be close.

I smiled as I looked around the cheerful yellow kitchen with an old avocado colored stove and worn cabinets. I had so many happy childhood memories in this place. My mother and I would spend summer afternoons in this kitchen, chatting with my grandmother as she baked cookies. My mother taught me how to make a casserole in this kitchen when I was sixteen.

My phone rang and I walked across the small living room to answer it. The caller ID said it was Karina, my oldest friend.

"Hello," I said warmly into the phone, expecting to hear my friend's voice.

"Aunt Hannah!" a small girl squealed instead. It was Leigh Ann, Karina's six year old daughter.

"Well, good morning," I said, a smile filling my face. "How's my favorite goddaughter doing today?"

"I'm good," she replied. "I wanted to make sure you were coming to the BBQ today. Mom said she wasn't sure."

"Of course I'll be there," I promised. "I wouldn't miss it."

"Good, because I miss *you*, Aunt Hannah," Leigh Ann said. "I want to see you."

My heart melted and it was all I could do to not tear up. "I miss you, too. I'm looking forward to seeing you today. Maybe we can play horseshoes."

"Yay! Horseshoes!" Leigh Ann squealed. "Mom! Aunt Hannah said she'll play horseshoes with me."

"That's great, honey." I heard Leigh Ann's mom, Karina, in the background. We'd been best friends since the third grade, when we snuck frogs into Mrs. Stone's lunchbox.

"Can I talk to your mom real quick?" I asked Leigh Ann.

"Yeah, here she is," Leigh Ann said.

A moment later, Karina came on the line.

"Hey," she greeted me. "I hear you're in town, but I haven't seen you for more than five minutes."

I chuckled, knowing that we'd stayed so long in a restaurant we were kicked out just a week before. Still, for being in town, I hadn't seen my friend as much as I would have liked.

"I know, and I'm sorry. I'm still getting settled," I said. "I think I'm finally settled in at work. We'll do something soon. Promise."

"Good. I need some more wine time," Karina replied. "Leigh Ann, do not climb on the counter tops. If you need to climb something, you can go outside."

From the background I heard a "but, Mo-om," followed

by a brief pause and then the sound of the backdoor opening and shutting.

"How long until summer is over?" Karina asked. "I don't know if I'm going to make it."

"It's barely June," I replied with a chuckle. "She driving you crazy already?"

"Yes. Her kindergarten teacher was a saint. I can't wait for her to start school again."

"She's going to be in first grade this year, right?" I asked, shaking my head. I couldn't believe my little goddaughter was already in first grade. It felt like just yesterday that she was born. I was one of the few people that Karina had wanted in the delivery room, and was one of the first to meet Leigh Ann.

"Yup. She's so excited for the full day, but I'm thinking I'm looking forward to it more," Karina joked.

"You realize in two years, Leigh Ann will be the same age that we were when we met?"

"My God, that's scary to think about," she said, laughing. "I really hope she doesn't pull the frog stunt. I was grounded for a month after that."

"Yeah, me too," I said. "Worth it though."

"Definitely. Seeing that mean old teacher scream was awesome." She laughed and let out a nostalgic sigh. "Anyway, do you want me to bring anything specific to the BBQ today?"

"I can ask my parents, but I'm guessing that you don't need to worry about it," I said. "They'll probably have tons of food and drinks. Maybe bring some chips and salsa if you have some."

"I can do that," she said. "Well, I don't need to keep you on the phone since I'll being seeing you in a couple of hours. Just wanted to hear your voice since I've almost forgotten what it sounded like."

"Very funny. We both know you couldn't ever forget my voice," I said. "But yes, I'm looking forward to seeing you guys today."

"Me too," she replied. "And I know Leigh Ann is. All she has been talking about all week is how excited she is to see her Aunt Hannah."

"Aw, that's sweet," I said. "Tell her I can't wait to see her, too."

"Will do," Karina said. "Oh, hey. I heard Dr. Matthews might come. Is that true?"

My heart skipped a beat at his name. "I haven't heard, but I did invite him."

"I wanted him to check this bug bite on Leigh Ann," Karina explained. "It's just so red."

"I'll make sure to take a look at it," I promised. "If it's bad, I'll let you know."

"You can do that?" Karina asked.

"I'm a nurse, so yes." I shrugged.

"I didn't know you knew stuff like that," Karina replied.

"Why do you think I went to school for four years?" I asked, rolling my eyes. "I don't just wear a short skirt and say 'thank you, doctor' in a breathy voice all day. I actually know medical things."

"Whoa, sorry." I could hear Karina take a step back. "I didn't mean to insult you."

I sighed. "No, I'm sorry. It's just that everybody in town thinks I don't do anything. That I didn't get a crap ton of training and experience."

"We've just never had a real nurse like you before," Karina explained. "Dr. Matthews is lucky to have you. We all are."

"Thanks." I sighed again. "We good?"

"We're always good," Karina assured me. "Hey, is it weird to work with Dr. Matthews? I mean, you tutored him in high school and now he's your boss."

"He's changed since high school," I told her. "He's not a punk kid anymore."

"Thank heaven. Remember when he punched out Aiden for drinking all his booze at that after party?"

"Yeah." I shook my head. It seemed like Jacob Matthews was always in trouble when we were in school. If you wanted booze or a party, he was the guy to go to. He had been trouble back then.

"He's a lot better now. There's no way I'd let him touch my kid otherwise," Karina agreed. "Okay, I'll see you in a couple hours. Thanks for looking at the bite. "

"Anytime."

She hung up the phone and I did the same. I walked over to the kitchen and poured myself a cup of coffee. It was good and warm in my hands as I took a sip.

I looked out my window and toward town. My thoughts went to Dr. Matthews and how much he'd changed since high school. How much we'd both changed.

I wasn't quite such an ugly duckling. He wasn't the bad boy. I let my thoughts drift to the first day that we really talked. The first day that my crush went into overdrive.

# CHAPTER 3

*Fifteen Years Ago: Riversville High School*

"You're late, Mr. Matthews."

I peeked over the top of my book to see Jacob Matthews saunter into Mr. Elway's classroom. He had on a black leather jacket, tight jeans, and a careless grin.

"So add it on to my time," he replied nonchalantly, spinning a chair to sit backwards at one of the classroom tables.

Mr. Elway sighed. "You have no idea how much I'm bending the rules for you. I don't allow students to retake the exams, but your parents..."

"Yeah, yeah. My parents." Jacob rolled his eyes. "My mom is on city council and my dad's the police chief. They get what they want."

"Yes." Mr. Elway adjusted his tie. He always wore a dress shirt and tie to teach class. No other teacher dressed up like he did. They didn't need to in a small town, but Mr. Elway wanted the best for his students. "Your parents have convinced me to make a special case for you."

Jacob shrugged and looked bored. My book lowered slightly as I tried to get a good look at him. As the nerdy goody-two-shoes, we weren't exactly going to the same social parties. We technically had gym class together, but Jacob almost never came. He almost never came to any of his classes, where I went religiously to everyone and as many academic activities as I could fit.

I was fairly sure that he didn't even know I existed. He was gorgeous. I was plain. My hair was cut too short and it frizzed terribly any time there was a hint of humidity. With summer only a month away, my hair was full on Bozo the clown.

I tugged on my shirt, wishing I hadn't had that extra cookie with lunch. I was terrible at sports, so marching band was the only physical activity I really had and the season had ended in November. It was May. As a result, I was on the chubby side. My mother promised me that I'd grow out of it, but I'd been hearing that promise for the past four years. I was beginning to doubt it.

"So what do you want me to do?" Jacob asked with a shrug. "You are the only teacher that isn't passing me."

"I pass those that do the work," Mr. Elway replied. "The others may let you off, but I see greatness in you. You're smarter than you let on."

"If you say so, professor." Jacob managed a cool shrug, but for a moment I thought I saw something cross his face at what Mr. Elway had said. I wasn't sure if it was fear or pride. "You still haven't told me what I'm doing here."

"The work," Mr. Elway replied. He motioned to a table at the end of the classroom. I'd spent the last twenty minutes setting it up as Mr. Elway's classroom assistant. There was a microscope and slides as well as some plant spores to look at.

"You'll make up every lab and every test if you want to pass the class."

Jacob looked at the microscope and looked completely unimpressed. "I didn't learn it the first time. What makes you think I'll learn it this time?"

"You didn't bother to show up the first time. And this time, Miss O'Leary will be teaching you," Mr. Elway informed him. "She'll be making sure you pass."

My eyes went wide and I dropped my book with a thud.

This was supposed to be my free-study hour. I was Mr. Elway's classroom assistant, not a teacher. I was supposed to help him grade papers and set up labs for the upcoming classes, not show the hottest bad boy in school how to use a microscope.

Jacob turned and looked at me, the full weight of his blue eyes hitting mine. He was so damn handsome it wasn't fair. I blushed hard and wished I could just sink beneath the desk and die.

"Hannah, you set up the lab. You know how it works." Mr. Elway motioned to the microscope. "I have a meeting. I want a full report when I get back."

"Wait, you're not going to be here?" I squeaked. I wasn't prepared for this. If I had known, I would have worn a totally different outfit. I would have attempted to do something with my hair. I would have been violently ill and missed the day entirely.

Mr. Elway picked up his suit jacket from the back of his chair and smiled at me. "You can do this. If anyone can, it's you."

He gave me a warm smile and left the room.

I was alone in the biology classroom with Jacob Matthews. This was something that I'd dreamed of but never dared even think it might actually happen. He was the hot bad boy. I was the geeky good girl.

I took a deep breath and tried to steady my nerves. I stood up and walked over to the lab table, frantically trying to remember exactly what was in this lab. Five minutes ago I knew, but that was before I had to explain it to Jacob.

"Okay. Um, I guess we should get started. We'll start with orienting you to the microscope," I said, hoping that I sounded more confident than I felt.

"What makes you qualified?" Jacob asked, his blue eyes looking me up and down. I felt exposed and far too big for the room when he looked at me.

"Other than Mr. Elway putting me in charge?" I asked, crossing my arms. "I passed this class two years ago. I passed AP Bio last year. I've spent the past semester helping teach this course to sophomores. You're a senior. How come you have to take bio?"

He watched me for a moment, his expression blank as he evaluated me. Then he shrugged. "I need one more science class to graduate. Mr. Elway didn't pass me, so I have to retake it."

I nodded. "Okay. That makes sense."

"Can you just pass me? Tell Elway that I did an okay job?" He put his hands in the pockets of his leather jacket. "I'll pay you if you want."

I frowned. "You can't *buy* me. You're gonna learn this."

His eyebrows raised. "And you're gonna teach me?"

"Yeah. It's not like Brock the Jock is gonna walk in here and teach you about mitochondria."

He rolled his eyes. "This is so stupid."

"It is not," I replied. He looked up surprised at the force in my voice. I was rather passionate about biology and learning. I loved biology. "It's not stupid."

"Says you."

"Biology is basically the study of sex," I told him, remembering something I'd read online. I had no idea where I was getting the courage to be sassy from, but I wasn't going to back down now. "I thought you'd be better at it than that."

"Whoa, whoa, whoa." Jacob held up his hands. "The nerd has some fire."

I crossed my arms and glared at him."I'm not going to lie to Mr. Elway."

He leaned back in his seat. "You said it was about sex? How is a microscope like sex?"

I was just glad he didn't ask me how someone like me would know about sex.

"How about you look in it and find out," I replied. "This lab is all about plant spores. You get to watch plant sex."

"You into that voyeurism, nerd?" Jacob asked. My face heated. I was sure that I was going to be a vibrant shade of red for the rest of my life.

"Just look in the microscope," I replied.

He chuckled and rose gracefully from his chair and sauntered over to the lab area. "Show me what to do."

He flashed me a wink that somehow made me turn even more red, but I wasn't about to let him get the best of me.

"You have to say that to women a lot?" I asked, plugging in the microscope and handing him the first slide.

Jacob laughed, the sound making my heart flutter. Good lord, how was I going to survive teaching him everyday?

"I like you, nerd," he said. "Show me your sex stuff."

I grinned, finally feeling like I might actually be okay with this arrangement. There was no way he would ever be my friend, our social circles were far too different, but for this hour, I thought we might get along.

I glanced a quick look at him, taking in the slim build of his shoulders in the leather jacket and felt my newly discovered interest in guys start to flare. If nothing else, I was going to have a hell of a story to tell my friends. I was tutoring Jacob Matthews.

I smiled as I remember that first day together. I'd tutored him the rest of the month. He was so smart. Once he got the core concepts, he flew through the material. He was actually really good at it, which surprised me given his attitude.

What surprised me even more was that we'd become friends. He laughed at my nerdy jokes. We talked a lot during those lessons, and not just about biology. He'd told me how he hated the control his parent's had in his life. They had forced him to take extra classes, so he'd failed them on purpose. His parents had just paid off the teachers.

I'd told him how I wanted out of this town. I was getting ready for college and leaving Riversville behind. I wanted to go to nursing school and see the world. He told me he had similar plans, but wasn't sure on the college side. I remembered blushing when I told him that he was definitely smart enough for it.

He'd kissed me at graduation. It was behind the bleachers after the ceremony once our parents had grown tired of pictures. He'd pulled me back there and kissed me without saying a word. One small kiss on the lips that set my entire body aflame. I'd never been kissed before that.

"Bye, Hannah." That was all he said after that. He left the next day and I hadn't seen him since. I'd thought he'd forgotten about me entirely. I followed him from a distance, checking in on him through social media and the gossip around town when I came home for the holidays.

Apparently, he'd gone to college and gotten a degree. He'd found himself once outside of his parents' reach. And then he went to medical school. He'd completed his residency in Denver before returning to Iowa to take over the town practice.

He'd been back in town much longer than me. Despite the

fact that it was a small town and everybody knew everything about everyone, no one knew much about Dr. Matthews' personal life. He'd managed to keep things quiet so far.

What I did know, were the things I'd heard through my mother and the Ladies' Bridge Club grapevine. He'd supposedly met a woman in medical school and had fallen in love. The story I heard, though, was that in the same week he'd planned on proposing to her, he also found out that she had been cheating on him. A broken heart was what had led him to move back to our hometown.

Which led to the two of us working together...

Regardless of the stories and the gossip, I still couldn't be certain whether or not he was officially single at this point in time. My mother seemed to think that he was going to marry Katie Jones. She was certainly beautiful and wonderful enough for him. She ran the bakery in town, and was the Ladies' Bridge Club's favorite single lady. I hadn't actually seen them together, but that didn't mean they weren't an item. Even though I'd come a long way from my ugly duckling stage in high school, he was still out of my league.

*Whatever, though,* I thought. *It's not like it matters. Nothing could ever work out between us either way. A doctor dating his nurse? No way. It wouldn't end well.*

Besides, he'd never tried to contact me after graduation. My friend invites had gone ignored. He wasn't interested in me. He was the rock star of the town now, and everyone expected him to marry Katie. I wasn't even on his radar.

I finished doing my hair and makeup, then went to my closet and pulled down some of my favorite outfits. The weather was supposed to be gorgeous today, so I decided to wear my favorite white summer dress. It had images of red and yellow flowers embroidered on it and it also happened to fit better than any of my other dresses.

After slipping it on, I faced the floor-to-ceiling mirror that hung on the back of my bedroom door. As expected, I was satisfied by the way it looked. It clung nicely to my hips and made my cleavage look good. It wasn't too revealing, but enough to make me feel sexy.

I wanted to look my best in case Dr. Matthews decided to take me up on my invitation to the BBQ. It was a fifteen year crush, but I couldn't put it behind me.

# CHAPTER 5

After taking the five minute drive across town, I pulled through the gate and down the paved driveway that led to my parent's house. Their land was immaculate. My father maintained every square inch of the acre around his house with amazing diligence. The grass on either side of the driveway was trimmed better than a soldier's haircut and the fence the surrounded the home was spotlessly white. My dad took pride in a well-maintained home. He always said that "Your home is the best representation of yourself."

If that saying were true, then I wondered if I actually was a small and rickety old woman whose hinges creaked when the wind blew, just like my house did.

I was surprised to see how many cars were parked around the house. I knew there were going to be a fair amount of people, since these gatherings grew every single year. However, I didn't expect this many. There must have been thirty cars on either side of the driveway, which had become overflow parking because the spots around the house were already taken up. There were even two tractors parked along with them. For a couple of people in town, their tractor was their favorite source of transportation.

*This is nuts*, I thought, parking at the end of the line of cars. *This has to be some kind of attendance record, I think.*

When I got out of my car, the sweet smell of home cooking entered my nostrils. I could recognize everything that my parents had on the grill using only my nose. There were burgers, ribs, pork and of course, corn. In Iowa, corn was a staple. It was rare to eat a home cooked meal and not have some form of it on your plate.

Also in the air was the sound of a banjo and drums. My parents had mentioned having one of the local bands come and play at the party, and they had apparently kept their word on it. But even louder than the band was the familiar roar of kids laughing and playing.

The sunshine poured over my fair skin as I made my way down the driveway toward the house. I was glad I'd put on sunscreen and had more in my purse. I went straight to the backyard. All I had to do was to follow my nose to figure out where the food was being served. When I turned the corner, my jaw practically hit the grass.

I could see families from all over town. There had to be well over twenty different families, all of them with a gaggle of children. It was a good thing my parents had a large yard because we never would have fit otherwise.

Dad was standing in front of the grill, carefully turning burgers over the flames. He was surrounded by five of his buddies, who were all chatting and laughing while they drank beer. My mom was at the opposite side of the yard. She was running around with a group of kids who appeared to have pulled her into an intense game of tag. The rest of the grass was covered with other neighbors and their families. I had never seen this many people in my parent's yard.

I'd hardly taken three steps toward the party before I felt

something wrap around my leg. I squealed in surprise when I looked down to see Leigh Ann's bright blue eyes gazing back up at me.

"Aunt Hannah, you made it!" she said with the kind of energy and excitement that I wasn't sure if I was capable of mustering up even on my best of days.

"Hey, beautiful girl." I picked her up and spun her around in a circle, letting her feet fly out away from me. "I missed you."

She giggled loudly until I stopped spinning. "I missed you, too, Aunt Hannah. Mommy's right over there. We were building a castle in the sand box. Do you want to help?"

"Yes, I definitely do," I said. "Give me a few minutes, though, okay? I just got here and want to say hi to my mom and dad."

"Okay, that sounds good," she said, her face beaming with happiness.

I set her back on the ground and watched her scurry across the grass, making her way back toward the group of kids who had gathered at the sandbox.

I only made it a few more steps before my mom saw me.

"Hannah!" she said, waving me over. "There you are. Come over here."

I kicked off my sandals, letting the cool grass slide between my toes. Then I jogged across the yard toward where my mom.

"Alright, kids, I'm taking a quick break," Mom told them. "Zachary, you're It!"

She tagged a little boy near her and he instantly turned and began chasing the other kids.

"Who's winning?" I asked with a smirk.

My mom caught her breath and pulled me in for a hug. We were the same height and similar build. I got my curly hair from her, but my eyes from my dad. "They are. I've got forty years on them, though. Doesn't seem quite fair."

I laughed and squeezed her tight. "How are things going, Mom?"

"Things are slow," she said, releasing me from the hug. "Slow and uneventful. Just the way your father and I like it around here. How about you? How's work going at the clinic? You settling in okay?"

"It's great," I said, as we both started walking toward the other side of the yard where my father and his friends were hanging out. "I'm keeping busy over there, that's for sure. The time goes by quick when I'm at work. How's dad?"

Mom glanced around, making sure that no one could hear us. The kids were too busy playing tag and the other guests were crowded around the grill or near the music.

"He nearly fell this morning." Mom's voice was quiet. "He's fine. He told me not to tell you, but..."

I wrapped my arm around my mother's shoulders. "Thanks for telling me. I'll make sure to check him over. I'm sure it's something simple."

Mom nodded, her eyes going to her husband. There was a quiet sadness to her that I'd never seen before. She took a deep breath and then shook herself. Suddenly, she was back to the bright cheerful woman everyone knew my mother to be. I admired her strength in the face of losing her partner.

"Have you said hello to your father yet?" she asked, taking my arm and guiding me toward the grill. "He is trying this new marinade and it sounds absolutely amazing."

Everyone rotated through various picnic tables and chairs positioned in the yard. There were too many families for everyone to eat all at once, so we took turns. I chose to eat with my parents and we all sat at the large picnic table under a sycamore tree. My mom was to my left and my dad was across from me. My best friend, Karina, was on my right. I decided I would stay close to family, rather than risk having to eat with Abigail St. James or some of the other popular girls that never left our town. I didn't need to be reminded of what I didn't have.

"It's nice to see you again, Hannah," Dad said, settling into his seat. "You should come by more often. You know we only live five minutes from you."

The sun reflected off of his bald head and lit up his red beard. He smiled and I knew I would hear that phrase from him many more times.

"Sorry, Dad," I said, as I buttered up my grilled corn. "I'll try to be better about it. You know how it is, though. If you're busy, you're busy."

"That's true," he said. "We're happy to have you here. What's new on your side of town? Dating anyone?"

I forced a smile and looked around the table. All of our family and friends were listening in on the conversation. They were staring at me, waiting for a response. I felt my cheeks heat and I knew that I was blushing.

"No, Dad," I said, through gritted teeth. "Still single."

My mom's good friend, Cynthia, decided to speak up. She was a nice enough lady, but didn't seem to have the mental filter, the one that separated her brain from her mouth, that most people did. She said whatever was on her mind and lacked a little thing called 'tact'. She was a top member of the Ladies' Bridge Club.

"When are you going to have a kid, Hannah?" Cynthia asked, pushing her sunglasses up on top of her head to get a better look at me. "You know, time waits for no one."

"Thanks, Cynthia," I said, with a bit of sarcasm. I was now

regretting my choice of seating. I would have been better sitting next to Abigail.

The worst part wasn't that she asked the question. It was that she felt the need to ask it in front of everybody and put me on the spot. I'd already felt embarrassed enough by my dad doing it, but Cynthia's question was even worse.

"I just haven't met the right guy yet," I said, shrugging my shoulders. "That's all."

Cynthia stared at me for a moment too long and I could tell she was judging me. She didn't say anything else, though, and eventually went back to eating.

"Has anyone seen Katie?" Karina asked, changing the subject for me. "I thought she'd be here."

Finally, after what felt like an agonizing eternity, Cynthia answered.

"No, she's working at the bakery today. She's got her baking competitions coming up so she'd been practicing like crazy."

"That's too bad," my mother replied. "I always like having her here. I am excited about her being on that baking show, though. It's going to be so exciting to have someone from our town doing something amazing."

Everyone began talking about Katie's new baking TV appearance, and I was just grateful that the attention was no longer on me. I exhaled a sigh of relief and the blood finally drained from my cheeks. I didn't mind being the center of attention, but I didn't want it to be because I didn't have kids.

Karina leaned toward me, whispering in my ear. "Just ignore them, Hannah. You know how it is in this town. People think you're from another planet if you're not married with children by the age of twenty."

I nodded in agreement. "Yeah, no kidding."

*I'm starting to wonder myself if I'm from another planet, though,* I thought. *I sure do feel like it sometimes. Maybe an alien from my home planet will come down and deliver me a kid if I pray hard enough.*

I ate the rest of my meal without saying much. The food was amazing and the company was good, I just wasn't in the mood for small talk any more. As I dove into my pulled pork, I gazed over toward the kid's table. There were at least ten children there and two of them were having a food fight. They were laughing as they flicked potato salad at each other using their plastic forks. Seeing it made me smile.

As much as I hated to admit it, Cynthia had been right when she said that time waits for no one. Time was passing and it was passing quickly. My body wouldn't be thirty-something years old forever and the longer I waited to have kids, the less likely it was going to happen.

I looked over at my dad as he laughed at something my mother said. It wouldn't matter how soon I had kids, though. My dad wouldn't get the chance to meet them. I'd have to get pregnant in the next few weeks just to have a chance, and the odds of that were beyond minuscule. I knew I couldn't adopt that fast either. Especially not as a single woman.

My thoughts were temporarily distracted when I heard the kids at the picnic table yell out with glee. They all shouted the same name with the kind of excitement that a child would have on Christmas morning.

"Dr. Matthews is here!" they called out. "Dr. Matthews is here!"

# CHAPTER 6

$\mathcal{I}$ nearly dropped my ear of corn onto the plate when I saw the most handsome man I knew walking around the corner and into the back yard. Sure enough, the kids were right. The good doctor had shown up to the party. He strolled across the grass, waving at the kids as he moved. I didn't get to see him in regular clothes very often, but when I did, I was always reminded of how good he looked.

He was wearing a simple red polo shirt with dark jean shorts and flip flops. The outline of his muscular chest was easily visible and the sleeves of his shirt were short enough so that his biceps were exposed. The kids all got up from their picnic table and swarmed around him, hugging his legs and squealing with joy.

"Hey, kids," he said, ruffling up their hair with his hands. "Are you guys having fun?"

"Yes!" they shouted in unison. It was almost as if they'd choreographed the whole thing. It was so damn cute.

"Good!" he said. "I'm so happy to see you guys."

After saying a few more words to the kids, Jacob strolled over to our table. Our eyes met and he smiled.

"Hey, Hannah," he said, his voice calm and soothing.

"Hi, Jacob," I said. "I mean, uh, Dr. Matthews."

He laughed softly. "Call me Jacob. You know that."

My dad spun around and gave Jacob a firm handshake from his seat. "Dr. Matthews is at our party? Well, this is a fantastic first. Glad to see you, Doc."

"Happy to see you, too, Frank," Jacob said. "Hannah told me about the party yesterday and I figured it was too nice of a day not to spend outside with you all. Plus, I could smell this amazing food from all the way at my house."

"Let me fix you a plate," Dad said, hopping up from his chair. "Have a seat, Doc."

Jacob took an open seat next to my dad, which put him directly across the table from me.

"Thanks for coming," I said, shifting in my seat. "I wasn't sure if you'd make it, but I'm glad you did."

"Thank you for inviting me, Hannah," he said. "It's nice to see you outside of the office once in a while."

I swear I thought he did an up and down of me with his eyes and then smile. But, there was no way that my boss would do such a thing. Still, it made me glad I'd worn the cute dress today, even if the once-over was all in my imagination.

It didn't take long before the rest of the table started talking to the doctor. I'm sure it was a common occurrence. Being one of the two doctors in town meant that he was bombarded with health questions constantly. I admired his patience, though, as he spoke with everyone there. His demeanor was so relaxed and happy, which was pretty much the opposite of how I had been feeling before he'd shown up.

I watched him dreamily as he spoke and only stopped when my mom nudged her elbow into my side.

"Hannah," she said. "Earth to Hannah."

Embarrassed for my staring, I turned away from Dr. Matthews and faced my mom.

"Hey, sorry, I was just listening to the Doctor," I said.

She glanced across the table to Jacob and then back to me with a frown. "I can see that."

"What's that supposed to mean?" I whispered.

"He's practically engaged to Katie," my mother whispered. "At least according to his mother."

"Practically isn't actually," I reminded her, repeating back a phrase she used to say to me all the time. "And he and his mother don't exactly get along."

"What makes you say that?" Mom asked, a frown creasing her brow.

I thought back to our high school days and just how much Jacob hated his mother. I wasn't going to tell my mom about that time though. She'd just say it was too long ago to count anyway.

"In the month I've worked at the office, I haven't seen Katie once. I haven't even seen things from her bakery, or even heard him mention her or the bakery," I told her. "If they were practically engaged, don't you think she'd have stopped by at some point?"

"Dr. Matthews is a busy man, and love works in mysterious ways," my mom replied, raising her chin. She looked over at Dr. Matthews talking to another guest and shook her head. "I love you, but he's not the man for you."

I sighed and picked at my corn. "Thanks, Mom."

My dad came back from the grill with a plate covered in food. He set it down in front of Jacob.

"Now this looks incredible," Jacob said, eyes widening. "Thanks, Frank."

"Of course," Dad said. "Anything for the Doctor. We're just glad you made it to the party. Eat quick, though, because after this we're playing tag football. Aiden's on the other team, so we need a good quarterback, too. You in?

"Most definitely," he said. "Under one condition."

"What's that?" Dad asked.

"I want Hannah on my team," he said casually.

My eyes lit up. "Really? I'm not that good at football."

"It doesn't matter," Jacob said. "We make the best team ever at the clinic. I think that would apply to a football game as well."

"Alright, I'll play," I said, excited to spend some more time with him that wasn't in the clinic. "Count me in."

"Omaha, Omaha," Jacob called out as he stood behind me. "Blue forty-two..."

I was bent over in front of him, holding the football to the ground. My legs were parted just slightly, enough for me to crane my neck and look between them. I saw Jacob's hands hovering between my knees, waiting to accept the football from me.

*I'm enjoying being bent over in front of him right now way more than I should be*, I thought. I'd borrowed a pair of my mother's shorts, so I wore the dress like an over-sized shirt. Even though I was bent over in front of him, there wasn't anything to see. It was too bad.

"Hike!" Jacob yelled out.

I snapped the ball to him and then jogged forward. We had eight players on each team and half of them were kids. Jacob lobbed the ball to Zachary, who juggled it as he ran. He nearly dropped it, but managed to hang on. The adults on the other team chased him down, but were unable to catch him. In the first throw of the game, our team scored.

"Yes!" I said, giving Jacob a high five.

"Good job, as always, Hannah," he said.

It was of course just a football game meant for fun, but it was still nice to score some points, especially with Abigail's husband as the quarterback for the other team.

We played football all afternoon until the sun began to slide downward toward the horizon. By then, we were all exhausted. The adults were anyway. The kids had just as much energy as they did when I first got there.

After winning the last game 21 to 14, Jacob and I walked toward the picnic table. We sat down next to each other, facing outward toward the yard. We watched the kids run around for a bit. It seemed they were still hyped up from the football. The mass amount of fruit punch they'd drank probably didn't hurt their energy level either.

"That was fun," I said.

I sat close to Jacob, but not too close so that it was weird.

"Yeah, it was." He glanced over at me and smiled. "Thanks again for inviting me. It's nice to get out once in a while. Seems like most of my life is spent at the office and when I have any free time, I'm usually just trying to keep my house in order."

"Do you live by yourself?" I asked casually.

"I do," he said. He glanced over at me. "You seem surprised."

My eyes had widened and it must have been clear how shocked I was.

"I guess I kind of am," I admitted.

"I'm surprised that you didn't know that," he said. "Yeah, I live by myself. Well, it's me and my dog, Wilfred."

"I just didn't know," I said. "I guess I never asked. It's really none of my business, though. I just thought you were probably seeing someone."

"You mean like Katie?" he asked, raising his eyebrows.

"Yeah," I replied, feeling a little silly. "I heard that you were practically engaged."

He sighed and picked a discarded piece of corn from the table, tossing it to the ground for the ants. His face was dark and eyes somber.

"Practically engaged. My mom seems to think she needs to help out with my love life. Katie and I are friends. Not even friends, really. Acquaintances. We went on one date and neither of us wanted a second. But, that's not what my mother wants." He shook his head. "So she's told the whole town we're 'practically engaged.'"

"So not much has changed there," I said quietly. "Same as high school."

"Nope. Some things change and some stay the same. I just wish we got to pick which things changed." He leaned back and the warm night air ruffled his dark hair. I wanted to run my fingers through it, so I played with the fabric of my skirt instead.

"It's hard to believe we met in high school." My curly hair had fallen across my forehead and I reached up, pushing it back over my ear.

"It feels like a different life, doesn't it?" he said, leaning his head back to look at the sky. He let out a slow, contemplative breath. "Time sure does slip by. I still remember when we graduated."

"Me too," I said, wondering if he was going to bring up the kiss. My heart sped up. "If I recall, you were late for the ceremony. They were just about to start when I saw you sprinting across the field to get in line."

Jacob laughed. "Yep. I remember the principle saying something to me that day. Something along the lines of, "Son, you're going to be late to your own funeral."

"Yeah, well, you obviously aren't like that any more," I said. "I don't think you would have made it through medical school otherwise. I think you're one of the things that's changed."

"I was a completely different person then." He lowered his gaze and faced me. "We both were."

I nodded, hanging onto his every word. There was a fleeting moment of silence. In that moment, Jacob and I just looked into each others eyes. They were dark blue like deep ocean water. It was like a magnet drawing me toward him, drowning me in them. The attraction in the air was palpable and electric.

I thought about that last kiss behind the bleachers and wondered if I should be the one to kiss him tonight. I wanted to. He had just a hint of scruff on his chin and his lips were right there. It would be easy if I could just build up the nerve.

Jacob finally looked away and my mother's words rang in my head. *He's not the man for you.*

"Well, it's getting late," he said, standing from the table. "I don't know about you, but between the long week and those kids running me ragged during the football game, I'm bushed. I think I'll head home and get some sleep."

*Oh no,* I thought. *I hope I didn't make him uncomfortable somehow. I shouldn't have said anything about graduation. I shouldn't have even thought about the kiss.*

"Yeah, I can understand that," I said. "I'll probably hang out and visit my parents for a little while longer."

"See you Monday?" he said, raising an eyebrow.

"Have I ever missed a day?" I asked with a smirk.

"Not one," he said. "But it's only been a couple of weeks."

"I don't plan on breaking my attendance streak just yet," I said with a giggle. "See you next week."

Jacob smiled and walked back toward my parent's house. I listened as he said goodbye to my mom and dad, thanking them for the amazing food and the good time. The humid summer air was still warm on my skin. Fireflies twinkled in the darkness beyond the light of the party.

*Does he like me? I could have sworn I felt something there.* I thought. *It's all probably just in my imagination. It must be. It's probably just my girl crush flaring up. There's no way Jacob would ever see me as anything more than his nurse. He's probably forgotten all about that kiss.*

As much as my heart hoped that there could be a flickering chance of something happening between Jacob and me, I refused to allow myself to think like that. I knew better. He and I weren't meant to be together. If we were, it would have happened years and years ago, during a simpler time.

# CHAPTER 7

The weekend went by far too quickly and Monday morning was there before I knew it. Luckily, I loved my job, so it wasn't like it was the worst thing in the world to have to get up and go to work. I just wished I could have slept in a tiny bit longer, that's all.

When I got to the office, I parked in my usual spot, right next to Donna's big red farm truck. I got out and then glanced at my reflection in the window of my car, making sure that I looked okay before heading in.

I looked pretty good today. My curly hair wasn't frizzing too badly this morning despite the humidity, and it was mostly contained by my ponytail. I had light eyeliner and mascara on so that my blue eyes actually looked like eyes rather than getting lost in my face.

"Oh good Hannah, you're here," Donna said, as I stepped in through the front doors. The waiting room was empty, which never boded well. Empty waiting rooms meant that fate was going to give us emergencies.

"Good morning." I smiled a little apprehensively and

approached the front desk, leaning my elbows against it. "What's up?"

"Well, you couldn't have arrived at a more perfect time," she said, holding out a patient file for me. "We have emergency stitches in room three. It's Stephanie Myers' little boy. Put his hand through a glass table."

"Oh no!" I picked up the file and quickly scanned it. Ashton Myers was four years old. No known allergies, was up to date on all his shots, and already had his physical done to go to preschool in the fall. "I'll set my stuff down and go right on in."

I hurried back to my office and threw my purse in the chair. I knocked gently on the exam room door before carefully opening it. Sitting on the exam table was a little boy with big blue eyes and tear streaks running down his cheeks. His mother sat behind him, her arms wrapped around him protectively.

"Hannah, perfect timing," Dr. Matthews said, turning as I came in. "Mr. Ashton here is going to get a very special kind of band-aid. I already applied the gel. "

"Does it have Paw Patrol on it?" the little boy asked hopefully. He wasn't crying anymore, but I knew that was going to change as soon as we started working on his hand. Right now it was under a blood soaked towel.

"Not quite," Dr. Matthews told him. He sat down on the round stool as I washed my hands and then finished prepping a tray with tools and meds for the doctor. "These are special string stitches. You cut your hand really deep and we want to make sure it heals. So, I'm going to use my magic string."

The little boy's chin wavered. "Is it gonna hurt?"

The way he dropped his r sound made my heart break.

"A little, yes." Dr. Mathew held his hand out and I passed

him the needle full medicine for numbing. "But, I'm going to give you some medicine so it won't hurt very much."

He lifted the towel from the little boy's arm to reveal a large, deep gash on Ashton's palm. With a gloved finger, he touched the outside of the injury.

"Do you feel that?" he asked.

Ashton shook his head. "No."

"Good. That means that gel I put on it is working. Now, I'm going to use a needle to give you more medicine. It shouldn't hurt because of the gel, but if you're scared, you can close your eyes."

Ashton's eyes went wide and his bottom lip quivered.

"Dr. Matthews is really good at this," I assured him. "Stephanie, will you hold him tight so he doesn't move too much? If you're not good with the sight of blood or needles, I can do it."

"I'm okay. Tough farm girl," she replied with a weak smile. "I got him."

"Okay." I put on my gloves and held onto to Ashton's arm so he would hold still as Dr. Matthews injected the numbing medicine around the cut.

Ashton cried out and tried to jerk away. My heart clenched in my chest. I loved pediatric patients, but this was the worst part of my job. I hated having to cause them any pain.

"Ashton, which Paw Patrol is your favorite?" I asked him, moving so that I was more in his line of sight than his hand. "I like Everest."

Ashton whimpered, but his mom whispered in his ear.

"I wike Marshall."

"He's the dalmatian, right? The one with spots. What color is his helmet?" I could hear Dr. Matthews set the syringe down on the tray behind me.

"Meds are in. I'm going to clean it out," he said softly behind me.

"It's wed," Ashton replied. I loved the way he said his r's and l's as w's. Red became wed.

"And he's the clumsy one, right?" I made sure to smile and keep his attention. "He tumbles into that elevator and knocks everybody over. What's the tower called?"

Ashton smiled. "Yeah. The lookout."

"And Rider always says, yelp for…"

"Help," Ashton answered, a smile crossing his face. It quickly turned into a frown. "I wanna be done now, please."

I glanced behind me to see Dr. Matthews shake his head. I could see he had just finished cleaning out a couple of small pieces of glass and was about to start the sutures.

"We're about halfway done," I told Ashton. "You are doing fantastic. Can you tell me who else lives in the lookout?"

Ashton frowned, obviously not pleased that we weren't done with this yet.

"Tell her," Stephanie whispered in his ear. "I know you love telling everyone about Zuma."

"Which one is Zuma? Is he the construction pup?" I asked, knowing full well that he wasn't.

"No," Ashton replied frowning at me. "Wubble is the construction pup. Zuma is the water pup."

He looked at me like I was the insane one for not knowing what dog cartoon characters did as professions.

"Oh. Tell me about him."

Ashton started slow, but built up speed as he told me of one of the many adventures Zuma and Marshall had been on. I quickly lost track of the plot, but it involved a whale. I nodded and made the appropriate surprised noises as he talked.

It wasn't long before Dr. Matthews touched my shoulder to let me know he was done. I let go of Ashton's arm and stepped back. The string of story coming from the boy didn't stop. He just started using both his hands to tell it.

His mom looked at his hand and she let out a relieved breath as she hugged her little boy tighter to him.

"Mom, I can't breathe." He squirmed in her arms.

"You did great, Ashton," Dr. Matthews told him. "I think you're the patient of the day. Would you like a sticker? Hannah will show you where they are while I tell your mom how to take care of your hand."

I leaned over and whispered, "We have Paw Patrol stickers."

His little face lit up and he wiggled out of his mother's grasp to take my hand. She gave me a smile as we left the door open and went to the front desk.

"Donna, we have a very brave patient who would like a Paw Patrol sticker, please," I said as we came to the front desk. "Actually, he was so brave, I think he can have three."

Donna spun in her chair and narrowed her eyes, assessing Ashton. "Hmm. I didn't hear any crying or screaming. Make it four."

Ashton grinned as Donna pulled out a roll of stickers filled with the bright dog cartoon characters. When his mom came out with Dr. Matthews, he had eight stickers- one for each character of the show. I gave him a high five on his good hand.

"Thank you so much, Hannah," Stephanie said as Dr. Matthews crouched down to talk to Ashton. "You made him so calm. If I didn't know, I'd say you had a dozen kids at home. Thank you."

She smiled and then took Ashton's good hand and headed home.

"Our next patient isn't until twelve," Donna informed us. "You guys are free for the next hour."

"Don't jinx it," Dr. Matthews told her.

Donna chuckled. "Eh, you have charting and stuff. Go get to work."

I went to my office to turn on my computer. There was a soft knock on my open door. I turned to see Dr. Matthews smiling in my doorway.

"Chalk up another success," he said, leaning against the door-frame and tucking his thumbs into his pockets. He looked good doing that. "Good job as always, Hannah. We made that look easy."

"That's always the goal, right?' I said. "He's a good kid."

"I'm more impressed at your Paw Patrol knowledge," he teased. "You watching cartoons on the weekends?"

I chuckled. "I used to babysit for the kid across the hall from me in Chicago. He loved that show. I know all the episodes."

"You did great. I haven't had stitches that easy in a long time." He smiled at me and my heart sped up at the compliment. "I'd let you take care of my kid anytime."

And suddenly I was imagining having kids with Dr. Matthews. My curly blonde hair, his blue eyes... It was so real in my mind.

"Thank you." I hoped I wasn't blushing too hard as I pushed thoughts of adorable Dr. Matthews babies out of my head. That was not work appropriate. "Anything you need from me right now? I'm thinking about grabbing lunch while it's quiet."

"No, nothing I need," he said. "Go have a good lunch and don't rush it. Like Donna said, we don't have any appointments for a bit. I'll call you if something comes up."

"I'd invite you to come with, but I suppose someone has to hold down the fort," I said.

"Yeah. I have to chart this," he said with a shrug. "Bring me back something?"

"Of course," I said. "What would you like?"

"Whatever you have is fine." Jacob pulled a twenty dollar bill out of his wallet and handed it to me. "I'll see you in a little while."

With that, he turned and walked down the hallway toward his office. I watched him all the way, admiring the way his butt moved underneath his slacks.

*He's your boss and not interested,* I thought to myself. *Knock it off.*

I didn't stop watching though.

I checked my work email and found that it wasn't anything that couldn't wait. There were definitely some benefits to a small town office. Things here weren't nearly as hectic or urgent as they were in the city. It was nice to know most of my patients on a personal level as well.

"I'm headed to Katie's Bakery to grab a sandwich and get some fresh air," I told Donna as I walked past her desk. "You want me to pick you up anything?"

She shook her head and lifted her lunch box up from the floor. "I brought my lunch today. Thanks, though, Hannah. See you when you get back."

I stepped out of the office and drew in a long breath of clean air. The air here smelled sweeter and cleaner than anything ever did in the city. The overcast sky provided some relief from the summer heat. Katie's Bakery was only a couple of blocks away, so I just walked there.

atie's Bakery was the best place in town to get sandwiches. And donuts. And cake. And really anything delicious. Katie had taken over the place after her father retired. She'd won a baking show on the Cooking Network last year, which was as close to famous as anyone in Riversville was ever going to get. She was now the town celebrity.

The bakery was also the only real place to get a take-out lunch that wasn't a burger or fast-food taco.

As I pulled open the door to the bakery, a familiar voice called out my name.

"Aunt Hannah!"

I turned to see little Leigh Ann and her mom, Karina, seated at a table outside. They were eating lunch on the patio right out in front of the Bakery.

"Leigh Ann!" I said. "What are you doing here?"

"Eating lunch with Mom," she said, matter of factly.

"Hey, Karina." I waived and Karina's eyes lit up when she saw me.

"Come sit with us after you order," she said.

"Yeah, definitely. Be right there." I ran in and ordered two turkey sandwiches on Katie's famous bakery rolls. They put one for me on a plate with a drink and one in a to-go bag with Dr. Mathew's name on it. Right as I finished paying, Katie the baker, came out from the back room with a tray full of fresh-baked rolls.

"Hannah? I heard you'd moved back, but I wasn't sure it was true or not," she said warmly, giving me a wave once she'd handed the rolls off to the sandwich-making employee. She had long dark hair and big brown eyes. There was a smudge of flour on her cheek and a speckling of it in her dark hair, making her look older than she was. She was six years younger than me, but I'd been friends with her older sister. To be honest, I'd gotten along better with Katie than I did her sister.

"Hi, Katie," I said with a wave of my own. "Yup. I'm back. I'm working at the doctor's office now."

"For Dr. Taggert?" she asked, coming around the back counter. We stepped off to the side of the checkout line, away from the flow of customers. She had on an apron covered in more flour and different colors of frosting.

"Kind of. He's selling the practice to Dr. Matthews. I work mostly for him," I replied.

"Oh, that's right. He bought it. I remember now." She shook her head and chuckled. "Honestly, I've been so busy the past few weeks it's a miracle I remember my own name some days."

"I've been watching you on TV," I said, feeling a little more confident that Katie and Dr. Matthews were no where near getting engaged. She didn't even know where he worked.

"Yeah, the baking competition. It was supposed to be this tiny thing and the network got ahold of it, and it kind of snowballed." She shrugged. "But, it's good for the bakery and the town. Mayor Matthews said tourism is up. The bakery's definitely been more busy."

"That's great," I told her. "I'm loving watching you. The finale is coming up, right?"

She nodded. "Filming is next month and it will premier a little after that. That's what I"m working on today. I'm practicing everything they might throw at me."

"Anyone going with you to LA for filming?" I asked.

"My dad. I don't have anyone else that really wants to go," she admitted. "Despite the Bridge Club's attempts, I am actually single."

"Be careful how loud you say that," I cautioned. "The town likes their romances."

"Tell me about it." She sighed. "I should let you eat your lunch. It's good to see you."

"Same. And in case I don't see you, break a leg at the competition."

"Thanks. Tell Dr. Matthews I said hi." She motioned to the to-go bag in my hand with his name on it, then frowned. "Actually, don't. I don't need to feed the gossip."

"I'll tell him you say a platonic hello and that you hope he enjoys his sandwich from a business standpoint as a returning customer," I said.

She laughed. "That'll work. It's good to see you, Hannah. I'm glad you're back in town."

She flashed me one last grin and a wave before heading back into the bakery area. I felt a little lighter knowing that she and Dr. Matthews weren't really an item. I knew that my thoughts didn't really matter, but it made my crush feel a lot less guilty.

When I stepped out onto the patio, Leigh Ann ran up and wrapped her arms around my leg.

"Well, this is a nice surprise," I said with a smile.

I set the sandwiches down onto the table and Karina and

I exchanged a quick hug.

"Hey there," she said, resuming her seat. "It's not often I run into you during the week. Everything okay?"

"Everything's great," I said. "Work is quiet today. We try and keep Mondays open for emergency visits since everyone waits through the weekend. I thought I'd grab some lunch since I didn't have patients."

"It was good timing," Karina said. "Leigh Ann and I just got here a few minutes ago. We were doing a bit of shopping and decided to grab some lunch."

"Thanks again for coming to my parent's party on Saturday," I said. "They loved seeing you and Leigh Ann. In fact, they sometimes refer to her as their 'step-grand daughter'".

Karina laughed. "You know I wouldn't miss it. I haven't missed one in twenty years and I'm not about to start."

I took a bite of my sandwich and washed it down with some orange-flavored bottled water. "It was nice seeing all of the kids play. They get along so well together. I wonder if they'll be friends two decades from now, like what happened with us."

"It wouldn't surprise me," she said. "They're thick as thieves. Speaking of connections, I noticed you and Dr. Matthews were hanging out quite a bit during the party."

I nearly choked on my sandwich from surprise. "What?"

Karina shrugged. "You and the Doctor hardly left each other's side the entire day."

"Oh, yeah, well." I stumbled over my words. "We've just become pretty good friends since we've started working together. Plus, I was the one who invited him, so maybe he felt like he needed to hang out with me more than anyone else."

Karina smiled and leaned across the table. "He's super cute, Hannah. You don't need to feel ashamed about having a crush on him."

"A crush?" I asked, feeling my face burn as I blushed. "What? No, it's nothing like that. We're just good friends."

"Okay," Karina said, keeping the mischievous smirk plastered on her face. "But I know love when I see it and there was definitely something there between you two."

"Do you really think so?" I asked.

"I know so," she said casually.

"Maybe you just had too much of the adult punch," I said, laughing.

"That's very possible," Karina admitted. "Even so, I wasn't the only one who noticed."

I cocked my head to the side. "What do yo mean?"

"Even your mom mentioned it," she said. "Right after Dr. Matthews left the party, she asked me if there was something going on between you two."

"Seriously?" I shook my head, causing my hair to fall across my forehead.

"It's not a bad thing," Karina said. "I think it's kind of hot. Think about it, Hannah. A nurse and a doctor? That's the kind of things they write books about."

"But the town..." I sighed. "Everyone thinks that he's engaged to Katie. Do you know what the Ladies' Bridge Club would do to me? My own mother told me to back off. They want him to be with Katie."

I motioned to the bakery behind us.

"Screw 'em."

I sighed. Karina had always been popular in school and the town adored her and Leigh Ann. She'd never felt the strength of the town when they decided on something. I had. I still had nightmares about Mrs. Thompson choosing me as the lead for the school play because it would bring me out of my shell. I had been so nervous that I had thrown up after every rehearsal and they finally gave up and let me just be in the band. The worst part was that I didn't even audition for the play.

When the town wanted something, it happened to you whether you liked it or not. The Ladies' Bridge Club was worse than the mafia.

"There's nothing between us," I told her firmly. "It couldn't happen and even if it could, I wouldn't allow it. He's my boss for crying out loud. You and I both know that mixing relationships with work is a huge no-no."

"I suppose," she said, before taking a sip from her cola. "Although, sometimes the heart wants what the heart wants. When that happens, I don't think there's much you can do about it."

"You got all this from seeing me hang out and play tag football one afternoon with him?" I asked, raising an eyebrow.

"Yep," she said confidently.

"Well, then you must be psychic or something," I said. "Or maybe *psychotic*. Not sure which. Because I don't think he wants anything to do with me that doesn't involve patients or their kids."

"Right." Karina rolled her eyes, obviously not believing me. "And you haven't thought about how cute a kid would be with your hair and his eyes. Or maybe his hair and your smile. Oh, that would be so cute."

*How did she know?* "Nope. Totally haven't, and you are delusional."

As if on cue, I heard the sound of a child crying. We both turned to look. It came from my left where a young mom was pushing a stroller down the sidewalk. I didn't recognize her and assumed she must have been from out of town. The mother stopped and checked on the her. She put more crackers in front of the girl, making the crying stop.

A little girl sat in her stroller smiling and carefully

picking up each cracker with tiny fingers before popping it into her mouth. Her hair was the color of Dr. Matthews' and she had beautiful blue eyes.

The image of a baby with Dr. Mathew's eyes in my arms popped into my brain again.

I was such a liar. I wanted a baby with Dr. Matthews. I wanted him. I wanted everything that I said I didn't.

I shook my head, knowing that I was fooling myself. It wasn't going to happen.

I was still feeling the effects of Ashton on my brain, I told myself. It always happened when I worked with kids. I couldn't get them off my mind. I wanted one of my own so badly, but it just didn't seem like it was going to happen. I was saving up to afford an adoption, but the idea of being a single mother was terrifying in a different way than not having kids.

"You, alright, Hannah?" Karina asked.

I realized then that I had been blatantly staring at the woman with the child. I nodded quickly, forcing my attention back toward Karina.

"Yeah, I'm fine," I said. "Sorry, just thought I recognized that girl."

"Oh, no problem," she said. "I was just telling you a funny story that happened to me at the grocery store the other day."

"Go ahead," I said. "I'm listening now."

Karina began to talk and I tried to pay attention. It was nearly impossible, though. All I could do was think about was a baby with Dr. Matthews' eyes in my arms. It seemed like everywhere I looked, women were having babies. Not just at my job, though, but *everywhere.*

*I need to have a kid and soon. Otherwise, I'm going to lose my mind,* I thought, while halfway listening to Karina's grocery store story. *I just need to find the right guy and it isn't Dr. Matthews.*

# CHAPTER 9

That night, I found myself completely exhausted. I ate a bowl of soup with some homemade banana bread and attempted to stay awake to watch my favorite reality show. Within minutes, though, my eyelids became heavy. I could hardly keep them open long enough to get up and turn off the television.

I somehow managed to find the remote, and once the television was off, I sat back down on the couch. I wrapped myself in a blanket that my grandmother had knitted for me as a graduation gift for getting through nursing school. My tiredness, combined with the warmth of the blanket, made me even more drowsy. As soon as I closed my eyes, I was asleep.

I had no clue how long I'd been out before a knocking came on the front door of my house. It was loud and sounded urgent, echoing off the walls. It caused me to wake up and wearily look around. When I glanced over, I noticed that the moon was shining its pale light through my windows.

*It must be at least midnight,* I thought. *Who could that be?*

After wiping the sleep from my eyes, I stood up from the couch and walked toward the front door. The knocking came again and I felt my heart leap into my throat. For a moment, I considered running to the garage and grabbing my old baseball bat. I didn't own any guns, so a bat was the closest thing I had for protection.

"Who is it?" I called out.

There was a second of silence and then I heard a man clear his throat. "It's me."

The voice sounded familiar, but I was still hesitant to unlock the door.

"Me?" I said. "That doesn't answer my question."

"It's Jacob," he said. "It's freezing out here. Can you let me in?"

My head cocked to the side in confusion.

*What's he doing here at this hour?* I thought. *He has never visited me at home before, let alone in the middle of the night. Why's he freezing? It's summer.*

When I opened the door, I saw Jacob standing there in street clothes. He had jeans on and a tight blue t-shirt, along with brown cowboy boots. His jeans hugged his hips in just the right places.

"Hey, is everything alright?" I asked.

It was then that I realized I'd answered the door wearing only my panties and a long t-shirt. I quickly pulled the bottom of the shirt down, using it to cover myself up the best I could.

"Yes, everything's fine," he said. "Can I come in?"

"Yeah, come on in." I held the door open for him, still confused as to why he was there, but also happy to see him.

As soon as I closed the door, he turned to face me. His eyes drifted down my body and then back up. His pupils seemed to dilate and I noticed it, despite the fact that the only light in the room was coming from the moon.

"I couldn't stop thinking about you." He stepped toward me as he spoke, quickly closing the gap between us.

"Dr. Matthews," I said. "Are you okay?"

"Never been better." He placed his hands onto my hips and took another step forward, pressing my back against the door.

Without saying another word, he leaned in and pressed his lips against mine. The kiss sent a burst of excitement through me. My heart was pounding behind my ribs. When he pulled away, the desire in his eyes became even more intense.

He brought his hands down my sides and around to my back. His fingers left a trail of heat across my skin. His kisses were hungry and his hands insistent.

"I need you," he whispered between kisses. "I need you so damn much."

Heat, desire, lust, and years of waiting all came to the surface. I wrapped my arms around his neck, plunging my tongue into his mouth. He moaned, driving me wild.

His hands slid up my shirt, palms against the bare skin of my stomach. He licked his lips, as his hand slid up my torso. I shivered as he inched higher and higher. He palmed my breasts, pressing his hips into mine. I could feel his desire and it was about to be mine.

"Yes," I whispered. They turned into a cry of pleasure. "Yes!"

My own words echoed through the house, startling me awake. My eyes opened and I looked around, suddenly confused. Dr. Matthews wasn't there and I wasn't even in the kitchen. In fact, I found myself laying on the couch. The TV flickered in front of me, playing some after-hours infomercial about a men's hair loss cream.

*Holy shit,* I thought, kicking the blanket off of me. *It was just a dream.*

There was a desperate aching between my legs unlike anything I'd ever experienced, though. The dream had felt so authentic, but now that it was over, my body felt empty. There was nothing more I wanted to do then to go back to sleep and resume the dream where it had left off. I closed my eyes, but couldn't seem to get tired again.

After a few minutes, I got up off the couch and went to the kitchen to make myself some tea. I tried to forget about the sexual images that my mind had created while I was asleep. It was difficult, though. I kept glancing toward the front door, somehow hoping that I'd hear a knock and find Dr. Matthews standing on the other side with that animalistic eagerness in his eyes.

The door remained quiet.

# CHAPTER 10

When I woke up the next morning, the vivid images from my dream of Dr. Matthews were still fresh on my mind. I could practically feel his kisses and the heat of his skin, even though it had never really happened. I got ready for work and noticed that I was in a surprisingly good mood. Even though it was the middle of the week and the weekend was still a few days away, I was humming to myself with glee.

If my city friends could see me, they would tell me I needed to get laid. If I was feeling this good off a dream, imagine what the real thing could do to me.

I spent the day feeling wonderful. The patients were happy, or as happy as they could be about being at the doctor's office, and I managed not to blush too hard around Dr. Matthews. The first encounter of the morning with him definitely threw me off my game, but I managed to not embarrass myself too badly.

The shadows in the office grew longer and the steady stream of patients trickled to an empty office. I sat at my computer charting the last few visits of the day and making sure that everything was ready for tomorrow.

"Well, this has got to be a first. I'm done before you are."

I swiveled in my chair to see Dr. Matthews leaning in my doorway. I would never grow tired of seeing him there. He had gray dress slacks and a dark polo on today. He'd taken off the white doctor coat and left it in his office, leaving him almost casual looking.

And of course, handsome as hell.

"That's because the last two patients were all me. I'm just doing your job for you," I teased, hitting save on the last patient file. "And you only beat me by a little."

He grinned and I suddenly thought of my dream. Heat flushed into my cheeks as I quickly turned to press the power button on my computer.

"What are you up to tonight?" he asked, his voice light.

I shrugged. "I'm going to go home and eat a can of soup and see if there are any new episodes of The Orville."

"It's a repeat. The new season starts in December," he told me.

"Damn. I hate summer TV." I heard my computer power down behind me. The office was quiet except for the hum of the air conditioner. We were all alone. I pushed dirty thoughts out of my head before they could fully form. "What are you up to?"

"I am not on call tonight, so I was going to go to Betty's Diner and getting a burger and a beer." He shifted his weight slightly, but kept the nonchalant lean on the door frame. "I was wondering if you'd be interested in joining me."

"Me?" I squeaked, not quite believing this was real. I half expected to wake up again just like last night.

"Yes, you," he replied with a grin.

"I'd love to." My heart fluttered and those dirty thoughts rose up yet again. Maybe we could have a couple of drinks and go back to my place, he could come inside... and I realized that I needed to slow down. "I mean, I don't want to intrude on your night and I know we're co-workers and-"

"If it makes you feel better, I asked Donna to come too," he interrupted. "She can't come because she doesn't want to leave two teenage boys home alone, and I can't say I blame her."

Heat filled my cheeks and I wished the air conditioning was just a little bit stronger. Or that the summer sky was just a little bit darker so that it wasn't quite so obvious. This wasn't a date. Obviously. This was a coworker thing. I was getting way too ahead of myself.

I blamed the dream.

"I would definitely prefer a Betty's Diner burger to my sad can of soup," I replied. "Thank you for inviting me."

He chuckled and I wondered if he suspected why I was blushing so hard. I really hoped he didn't know that I had a monster sized crush on him. That I had since high school, really, but working with him was just making it grow again.

"I'll meet you there," he said, pushing himself off the door frame. He flashed me a grin. "Last one there buys drinks."

"You're on." I grinned and grabbed my purse. Not that I thought my ancient car would win any kind of race, but I knew a secret route that would get me there first.

We managed to walk civilly out of the office. Dr. Matthews pulled out a set of keys and locked up after us. We both walked like adults to our vehicles, which is when I realized that Dr. Matthews' didn't drive his truck today.

"You drive a motorcycle?" My jaw dropped open as I stared at the chrome and black leather. It looked fast.

"I *ride* a motorcycle," he corrected, putting on his helmet. "How did you not know this?"

"I knew you rode one in high school, but it wasn't like

this." I motioned to the beautiful bike in front of me. "I thought you drove a truck now."

He shrugged. "Sometimes. But I like the bike better. Especially in the summer." He flashed me a grin before lowering the visor on his helmet. "You better get in your car if you hope to beat me."

I narrowed my eyes at him for a second before sprinting to my car. The locks chirped as I threw open the drivers' side door and mashed the key into the ignition.

Dr. Matthews revved the engine on his bike and peeled out of the parking lot. I slammed my car into reverse and followed behind him as quickly as I could. It was okay that he was ahead of me. He didn't need to know my shortcut.

I made a hard right on Elm while he continued down Main Street. I had this race in the bag. There was no way he knew about the new alley between Ash and Locust. They'd finished it two days ahead of schedule, so no one knew it was a route yet. I was already imagining the look on his face when he pulled into the diner's lot and found me waiting for him.

I turned into the alley and went as fast as I dared through the narrow space. I was going to win this race and get the most expensive drink on the menu. Which really just meant that there would be extra rum. There were no super fancy or expensive drinks at Betty's.

I turned into the parking lot to find Dr. Matthews leaning on his bike next to an empty parking space for me. He even had his helmet off. Somehow he had beaten me. I pulled into the spot and turned off my car.

"How did you beat me?" I asked, slamming my door shut.

"You took the new alley on Ash," he replied. "I took the alley on Cipher."

"There is no alley on Cipher Street," I said, frowning. There was a small space between the brick buildings, but it wasn't a road. It was basically just a place to store the business trashcans until trash day.

"There is if you're on a motorcycle." He grinned. "Car won't fit, but the bike goes everywhere."

My jaw hung open. I could imagine him weaving through the plastic trash bins on his bike. It was dangerous, but it had meant he won.

"I think that's cheating," I told him, crossing my arms. "That's not a road."

"Neither is the alley on Ash," he replied, his grin telling me that he knew he had me.

I scrunched my nose, trying to think of a way to disqualify him, but he had beaten me. "Fine." I let my hands fall to my sides. "I'll buy your drink."

"Excellent." He straightened up from his bike and grinned at me as we entered Betty's Diner.

Betty's was the local watering hole. To be honest, it was the only watering hole with food. Riversville was small, which meant that we had the bakery, the grocery store deli, a McDonald's, a Taco Bell, a pizza place that changed names every year but the pizza never changed, Rob's Bar, and Betty's Diner. If you didn't want to cook, the options were rather limited.

However, Betty's Diner had the best food. Even after living in Chicago, I could say that Betty's burgers were better than more famous restaurants. Her cheese curds were worthy of the state fair, and as long as it wasn't healthy, Betty's did it best.

We stepped inside and headed out to the open patio. Most of the patrons were inside enjoying the air conditioning and watching a NASCAR race on TV, leaving the patio to just the two of us. With the sun setting, there was a nice breeze and we got enough of the air conditioning coming out from the open doors to make the patio warm but comfortable.

"Dr. Matthews, Hannah." Stephanie greeted us and handed us menus. "It's good to see you."

"How's Ashton?" I asked, taking the menu.

"You'd never even know that he'd hurt himself," Stephanie replied with a laugh. "He's been running around catching bugs all day since I won't let him go swimming. He wants to go in the river so bad, but I keep telling him Dr. Matthews will be mad. It's the only thing keeping him dry."

"I'm glad to hear he's doing well," Dr. Matthews replied warmly. "He's a good kid."

"The best," Stephanie agreed. She grinned. "Although, I might be a little bit biased."

"I'll take a Betty burger with fries," Dr. Matthews said. "And Hannah is buying me a double whiskey on the rocks."

Stephanie raised her eyebrows at me and I sighed. "He beat me here, so I'm buying drinks. I'll take a whiskey sour and a Betty's burger, too."

"Did you not take that new alley on Ash?" Stephanie asked, collecting our menus.

"I did. But he's on a motorcycle," I told her.

"Oh. He took that trashcan alley on Cipher." She winked at the doctor. "I knew you were a smart cookie."

I just shook my head at the both of them.

She smiled and promised to bring our drinks out as soon as possible.

Dr. Matthews leaned back in his chair and took a deep breath in. "You know, I never thought I'd see you back here."

"Me?" I shook my head. "You're the one I didn't expect. You disappeared so fast after graduation that I didn't even get a chance to say goodbye."

Or ask you about that kiss.

"Yeah." His eyes went distant and I wondered if he was thinking about that kiss as well. "Sorry about that."

"It's okay," I told him. "But, why did you come back? I thought we were both free."

He sighed. "You want my whole life story?"

"Sure. Especially since I know the first eighteen years of it."

I thought of all our lab time together as I taught him biology. He was so quick to learn. It had started out with awkward silences, but with every class spent together we talked more.

I'd learned about how his parents had grand plans for him, but had never bothered to ask him what he wanted. He wasn't sure himself back then, but he knew he wanted out from under them. It was a big part of why he was always getting into trouble.

Dr. Matthews smiled and for a moment I caught a glimpse of the Jacob I once knew.

"Let's see. I got into a community college just outside of Des Moines and earned my associates there. Transferred to Iowa State, and got my bachelor's in biology."

"Biology?"

"You inspired me," he replied. His blue eyes crinkled in a smile. "So, thanks for that. Anyway, I went to Medical School. Did my residency in Denver. Got a job there. And I almost got married, but didn't."

"I'm sorry to hear that, Dr. Matthews," I told him. But I wasn't really sorry.

"Seriously, call me Jacob." He smiled that slightly crooked smile that had made my knees weak in high school. He'd only gotten better at it.

It was then that Stephanie arrived with our drinks and a basket of fried cheese. The conversation paused for a moment as she told us our burgers would be out soon and the cheese was on the house. We smiled and thanked her.

The hum of the cicadas thrummed as the sun slowly

made it's way to the horizon. Everything was awash in orange and yellow.

"So, what happened?" I asked, sipping on my drink and then picked up a homemade fried mozzarella stick. It was crispy and gooey and delicious. There were definite perks to being a favorite person in a small town.

He took a long sip of his drink.

"Her name was Diana. I met her my first year at the job and we hit it off. Two years later, we were planning a wedding." He picked up his drink and swirled the amber liquid before continuing. "I was fresh out of residency and didn't really have a good way to pay for the big wedding she wanted, so I started moonlighting at an ER in the city on days she worked. I didn't tell her that I was working there. The money was going to be a surprise."

I nodded, sipping my drink. I knew plenty of docs that worked two jobs. Medical school was not cheap. Those loans were hard to pay off.

"Anyway, one night this guy comes in with textbook appendicitis. The OR is backed up and the ER is slow for once, so we keep him and start the process. He's in a lot of pain, so I give him some meds since he signed consent."

I took another cheese stick and munched quietly, listening to his story. He took a deep breath.

"He starts telling me about his girlfriend. How amazing she is, how he's going to marry her, how great the sex is..."

I choked a little on my cheese and Jacob looked up. He raised an eyebrow to ask if I was okay. I took a sip of water and motioned him to keep going.

"He was high as a kite on the meds. I learned more than I ever wanted to know about this man and his girlfriend while we waited for her to arrive or the OR to open up. Girlfriend showed up first. Walked into his room and kissed him."

I could already see where this was going. "Oh no. It was Diana, wasn't it?"

"Yup. She tried to play it off, but she kissed him right in front of me. I had to go take a walk around the parking lot." His fist tightened and pain filled his blue eyes. "He was no longer my patient that night."

"I'm so sorry," I told him. I felt terrible for him. I could only imagine the pain of finding out that someone you loved was cheating on you behind your back.

"I ended it right there. As far as I know, she's still with appendicitis guy. I found out that a couple of people I thought were friends either knew about them or suspected. No one told me." He took a big sip of his drink. "That wouldn't happen here."

"No, it wouldn't. You can't even pick up a tomato at the grocery store without the gossip brigade announcing you're a vegetarian," I replied. There were some perks of the Ladies' Bridge Club being in everyone's business.

"I needed a change." He shrugged and picked up a bite of cheese. "And cheese. You can't get this stuff anywhere else. So, that's why I'm back."

I giggled and took another piece myself. "I'm sorry that happened to you."

"It hurt at the time, but I think I dodged a bullet. I took the money I'd saved up and started the process of buying Dr. Taggert out of the clinic. He's not totally ready to retire, so he likes giving me the lion's share of clinic hours and call time. I'm happy again. I don't have the stress anymore. Plus, I got to hire you."

"And I'm glad you did,." I smiled at him and he grinned back at me.

"What about you? Why are you here?" he sipped at his drink.

I shrugged. "Family. I liked the city, but I think I need to be here for awhile. I'll go back eventually."

"You're not planning on staying then?" he asked. I thought I might have detected a note of worry, but it was probably because I was an awesome nurse. He wouldn't want to lose me.

"Maybe a year or two?" I shrugged. "I'm just kind of playing it by ear. It's nice to be out of the city. It gives me a chance to build up some savings and see my folks. I miss them a lot. And, the cost of living is obscene in Chicago. You have no idea how much I'm saving just in rent."

He nodded slowly, spinning the whiskey glass in his hand. He looked thoughtful before saying, "You're here for your dad, aren't you?"

"I did say I was here for family, didn't I?" I asked, doing my best to give a nonchalant shrug. My dad didn't want the town to know he was dying. He didn't want them to treat him differently.

"You know I was the one who found his pneumonia the first time, right?" Jacob asked quietly. His blue eyes met mine and I could see a sad understanding. The chest x-ray had been the first sign of my dad's cancer. It had been the start down this terrible road.

"You know?" My voice cracked. I glanced around at the empty patio. "You didn't say anything."

"It's not my place," he replied. He took a sip of his drink. "I know he's glad you're here, though. He told me his care was in the best hands. And he is."

I opened my mouth, but wasn't sure what to say. Luckily, Stephanie pushed open the swinging door with a rush of cold air and the scent of grilled meat.

"Two burgers," she said, setting them in front of us. "Can I get you two anything else?"

"I think we're good," Jacob said, picking up the ketchup bottle. "Thanks."

"Holler if you need anything," Stephanie said with a smile before heading back inside.

I stared at my burger trying to digest what I'd just learned. Jacob had had his heart broken .Jacob knew about my dad. But, most importantly, he was definitely single.

"What about you?" he asked, mumbling around a bite of hamburger. He swallowed. "Is there a special someone in Chicago?"

"A what? Oh, no." I shook my head. "No, no, no."

He took a bite of his burger and raised his eyebrows waiting for more. I sighed and cut my burger in two so it would be easier to eat.

"There was a guy a few months ago, but it wasn't serious," I told him. "Turns out that he discovered he likes guys."

"That happens sometimes."

"Yeah." I took a big bite of burger and my mouth sang a happy little song. Betty's burgers were seriously the best in the world. "It's okay, though. It made the decision to move out here a lot easier. Being single's not so bad."

Jacob nodded, a small smile on his face. He quickly took a bite of his meal and smiled a little bigger. He must have been enjoying his burger. I know I was.

"To being single," he said, holding up his glass for a cheers.

"To being single." I clinked my glass against his and we both drank.

We sat in comfortable silence for a moment. The warm breeze drifted across my skin and I felt relaxed for the what felt like the first time in months.

*Coming home was definitely the right decision*, I decided. I felt a tension I didn't even realize I had melting out of my shoulders. I ate slowly, not wanting to hurry this moment. I wanted this time with Jacob to last for as long as I could.

"Tell me about Denver," I said, purposefully setting down my burger so I would have an excuse to stay longer. "I've never been. Is it good skiing?"

"In Denver?" He chuckled. "You don't ski in Denver. You have to drive two hours to get to the mountains to ski."

"What? I thought that was Denver's thing!"

"Nope. It's a city, and it's not even in the mountains." He shook his head and chuckled. "But, the view there is amazing. The mountains at sunset are breathtaking."

I grinned and leaned back as he told me about his adventures. The night grew darker around us and Stephanie came out and refilled our drinks at least twice, but I swear it only felt like a few minutes. It felt like those times in biology lab back in high school.

It was perfect.

# CHAPTER 11

The next day, the clinic was insanely busy. It seemed like everyone and their mother had some sort of medical complaint. I worked through lunch. I worked until my eyes were blurry and my stomach groaned with hunger. I snarfed a banana and some beef jerky between two patients just so that I wouldn't pass out from running around the office.

"Hannah? You have Emily in room four," Donna reminded me as I chugged a cold cup of coffee that I'd forgotten this morning. "She knows we're behind, but it's been thirty minutes. Remember to check on her."

"I'll be right in," I promised. "What other patients do we have?"

Donna glanced down at her list. "Dr. Matthews is just finishing up with one and then we're actually caught up. No one's on the list."

I stared at her for a moment. "Seriously?"

She nodded. "Everyone wanted to be seen as soon as possible. The rush is over."

"Thank god," I told her, finishing my coffee. "That

morning was brutal. I'm going to need the open afternoon just to get half the charting caught up."

"It's not even afternoon anymore." Donna nodded. "Full moon tonight. And there's a huge storm moving in this evening. It makes everyone all crazy."

I set my coffee cup down, made sure I didn't have any crumbs on my scrub top, and took two steps to the patient rooms before stopping.

"Why is Emily here? Her next appointment isn't for a few days."

Donna handed me a clipboard with Emily's neat hand-writing on the paperwork.

"She's been feeling some contractions and wanted Dr. Matthews to take a look. That's why she was willing to wait out the rush," Donna explained. "It's her first baby. She's nervous about it."

I nodded, taking the paperwork. "Thanks, Donna."

I carried the clipboard into the exam room. Emily was pacing the small space, but she stopped and smiled as soon as I came in. She wore the exam gown with her clothes neatly stacked on the chair beside her.

"Hi, Emily. I'm so sorry about the wait," I said, going to the sink and washing my hands. "It's been a crazy day."

"It's no problem," the young woman assured me. "Actually, I feel safer here than at home. Greg is out in the fields, and I don't want to be by myself."

"Tell me what's going on," I said, sitting on the small circular stool. It felt good to sit for a few minutes.

"Is it okay if I keep walking? It feels better if I'm moving."

"Sure," I told her with a smile. I looked down at her paperwork. "You said you're having contractions?"

"Yeah. I mean, I know I'm only at thirty-six weeks and I'm a first time mom, so they're probably just Braxton Hicks like the book says, but they just hurt so much..." She stopped and her face tightened as her body contracted. I could see the muscles across her stomach practically ripple under her exam gown.

There was no way those were "practice" contractions. Those were the real thing.

"How long has this been happening?" I asked, standing up and putting on a pair of gloves. All tiredness was leaving my body and getting replaced with adrenaline. If this was what I thought it was, my day was about to get even crazier.

"Um, since before breakfast. They're getting worse." She whimpered and closed her eyes as her hands balled into fists.

"Breathe," I coached, coming to her side. I waited until her eyes opened. "Okay. I need to check you. I think you might be in labor."

Her eyes went wide. "But I'm only at thirty-six weeks!"

"Which is considered full term, but still early," I assured her. "It'll take me two seconds to check."

"Okay." She swallowed hard and sat down on the exam table only to have another contraction ripple through her. It looked incredibly painful and was less than a minute from her last one.

When the contraction was over, she slid into place on the exam table and put her feet in the exam stirrups so I could check how dilated her cervix was. If she was anything over four centimeters, we would send her to the hospital, though given how closely her contractions were, I was ready to call an ambulance and send her to the hospital now. If I sped like a maniac, it was a good thirty minute drive to the nearest hospital.

"Oh boy," I whispered to myself. I checked my measurements and then double-checked. She was nine centimeters of the needed ten and ready to go.

There was no way she was going to make it to the hospital. I wasn't even really sure the ambulance would make it to the clinic in time.

"I'm not dilated at all, am I?" Emily asked, peeking over her knees at me. "My mother-in-law said I was just being dramatic."

I rolled my stool back and took off my gloves. I'd delivered plenty of babies at the hospital, but that was at the hospital. With lots of machines and medicines and tools. This was going to be a first for me.

"Emily, I need you to call your husband and tell him to get here as quickly as possible," I said, keeping my voice calm. She had another contraction and I felt like I should put my hands out just in case the baby popped out, even though I knew that wasn't how it worked.

"You're sending me home, aren't you?" she gasped once she recovered. "These are just the practice ones the book told me about."

I smiled and took her hand. "These are the real deal. You're going to have your baby today. Probably very soon."

Emily's eyes went wide and she froze for a second. She swallowed hard.

"Well, at least I don't feel like such a weeny. These contractions hurt like hell. I thought I was just being a wuss about them," she said after a moment.

"Nope. They're very real and you're doing great. Call your husband. I'm going to go grab Dr. Matthews," I told her, standing up and washing my hands. "If you get the feeling that you need to push, don't. Do not push without me in the room, understand? It's important."

"No pushing. Got it." She nodded her eyes wide. "Hannah?"

"Yes?"

"You're going to be with me, right? This wasn't the plan, and I'm scared." She bit her lower lip.

"I promise I'll be here for you. It's not the plan, but we're going to make it work. You've got this, okay?" I tried to sound more in control than I felt. The baby was technically full term at thirty-six weeks, but still way too early. The implications of what could be causing this early labor made my heart sprint, but I didn't want Emily to know my worries.

She nodded. "Okay. No pushing."

I gave her a quick smile before darting out of the room. My heart was pounding in my chest and my knees were shaking. Delivering babies in a doctor's clinic wasn't exactly in my job description.

The door next to me opened and Dr. Matthews stepped out with his last patient.

"Now, go check out with Donna and I'll see you in three weeks," he told the man. I recognized him as one of the farmers that was friends with my dad. He was a regular in the Gentleman's Poker Club. I gave him a polite nod as he passed.

"Thanks, Doc," he said, giving me a return head bob as a greeting.

"Crazy day, huh?" Dr. Matthews said, turning to face me with a smile.

"It just got crazier," I informed him. "Emily is nine centimeters and ready to push."

To his credit, the only indication that I'd just dropped a bombshell on him was a slight tilt of his head and a slow nod.

"Room four?" he asked. I nodded. "Okay, then. Tell Donna we need supplies. There should be a delivery kit in the store room. I want the chopper, too."

"You want a helicopter?" I asked, surprised.

"With a baby this early, anything can happen," he said, his eyes going serious. "You ready?"

"This is my first non-hospital birth," I admitted quietly. I didn't want Emily to hear me. It's never good to hear your nurse panicking.

Dr. Matthews smiled and put his hand on my shoulder. "Nothing like a first," he said with a smile. He gave me a reassuring squeeze and then knocked on the door to Emily's room.

I heard him greet her as I hurried to the front desk where Donna was chatting with the farmer. I came up and put my hand on Donna's shoulder.

"I'm sorry to interrupt, but I need you to grab me some supplies for a patient," I told her. "And Dr. Matthews wants HeliMed."

Donna frowned for a moment, did the mental list of what patients were here, and then her eyes went wide. "You need the kit?"

I nodded.

"Well, don't stand here gawking at me," she chided. She turned to the farmer. "Mr. James, you're all squared away. Tell your wife I said hello and I'll see her at the next bridge game."

She then picked up the phone and dialed from memory. "This is Riversville Clinic. We need a air evac."

I could hear a voice on the other line. She nodded and then put her hand over the receiver.

"They're fighting the storm. It's going to be at least thirty minutes."

I chewed on my lip. That wasn't going to be fast enough. "Have them come anyway, I guess. We'll figure it out."

She gave me a smart nod. "Well, don't just stand there gawking at me. I'll get you the kit as soon as they've given me confirmation."

I stood for a second, still trying to keep up with what exactly was happening. I gave her a nod and hurried back to Emily.

Dr. Matthews was coaching Emily through a difficult contraction. She moaned softly, fingers digging into the thin padding of the exam table.

Some women screamed. Some women cried. Some cursed. Some women went quiet. Everyone handled the pain of childbirth differently. I personally already knew I wanted an epidural and was probably going to be a screamer. Emily appeared to be the kind that went quiet.

"You're doing great." Dr. Matthews' voice was low and soothing. He emanated a calm and gentle aura. It wasn't his usual joking or his high school bad-boy vibe. It was the mark of someone that cared and was there to help. He was a true healer.

I washed my hands and was drying just as Donna knocked on the door. I answered and Donna handed me the pouches of medical supplies, several towels, and two surgical gowns and eye-shields.

"I'll bring back Mr. Markins as soon as he arrives," she told me. "I'll prep the rest, but that should get you started. Still thirty minutes ETA on the chopper."

Her calm confidence soothed my nerves. "Thanks, Donna."

"You'll get used to calling for the chopper," she assured me, making sure I had everything. "We call them more than you'd expect. Oh, I have the ambulance on stand-by as well."

It was a good thing to have an experienced secretary. It felt better to know that there was yet another person in the office who could help if things didn't quite go as planned.

I tried not to think of all the things that could go wrong. This baby was too early. What if the lungs didn't work? Why was the baby coming so early? There were so many terrifying things that could go wrong. I was glad there was a helicopter on the way. If things went south, we would need the speed of a helicopter.

I set the supplies down and started prepping things as Dr. Matthews kept Emily on task. The birth was coming on quickly. We both gowned up in the blue surgical gear, donning masks, gloves, and eye goggles. Births were known to get messy.

"Okay," he said after a particularly long contraction. "You're ready to push."

"Not without Greg," she gasped, her body preparing for birth. Sweat dotted her brow and her blonde hair stuck to her skin. "He promised he'd be here."

"I'm here," Greg Markins announced, rushing into the exam room. He had on his work gear and pieces of hay in his hair. "I'm here, baby."

Relief filled her face before another contraction hit. Greg gave her his hand and then immediately winced and regretted the decision as she squeezed hard.

"Perfect timing, Greg," Dr. Mathew told him, centering himself between Emily's legs.

I hurried around the room, making sure things were ready for the baby. In the hospital, there were two nurses for mom, two nurses for the baby, a pediatrician, and an OB. Today, it was me and Dr. Matthews with back-up from Donna.

It was definitely makeshift, but it felt like we were prepared. I'd done this hundreds of times, but this one felt special. There was an new urgency and a lack of control that made this one different than all the hospital births I'd assisted with.

"And push." Dr. Matthews voice was strong, yet compassionate. Emily grunted and squeezed her eyes shut, her knuckles going white with effort as she tried to bring her son into the world. "Good. Breathe. And push again."

I held a bulb syringe and a blanket, ready to do my part once the baby arrived. Dr. Matthews kept gently coaching, telling her to push and reminding her to breathe. It was a steady process, yet I kept holding my breath with every push.

I prayed that this went well. I'd seen emergency births at the hospital that I wouldn't want to recreate here. I prayed for an easy birth, one that was safe for both the mother and child. Having a baby was a dangerous thing to do. Just because most mothers survived in this century didn't mean it was safe.

"Hannah, we're ready," Dr. Matthews said quietly. He raised his voice. "Push, Emily. Push."

Emily cried out for the first time all afternoon. Her poor husband looked pale as a sheet as she gripped his hand. Emily strained and used all her energy to bring life into the world.

A moment later, I could see the baby's head in Dr. Matthew's hands. I could tell he was grinning like a lunatic, even under the mask. A birth was always an amazing thing. "I've got him, push again."

A slippery baby slid into his waiting hands and he quickly wrapped the child in a towel. Dr. Matthews' face went stony. The baby wasn't moving. There were no cries. The infant hung blue and limp in his hands.

"Suction," Dr. Matthews commanded. I came in and suctioned the little boy's nose and mouth, making sure that they were clear before he could breathe in anything that would make him sick. There was still no movement.

My heart was falling through the floor.

*No,* I thought, fighting back tears. *Not after all this.*

"Again." Dr. Matthews waited until I had cleared everything, and then began moving the baby around and vigorously rubbing the child's back.

Suddenly, the infant let out a strong shriek of anger at suddenly being cold, wet, having things sucked out of his mouth, and being rubbed. My heart moved out of my throat and I could breathe again.

Tears ran down Emily's face as I took the baby from Dr. Matthews, did a quick check to make sure he was well. He was now breathing normally and moving appropriately. He lost the frightening blue pallor and quickly pinked. Once I knew he was okay, I placed the baby on Emily's chest. She and her husband both held onto their small family, crying tears of joy. I watched them for a second, enjoying their joy, before focusing on the rest of the birth process.

Dr. Matthews continued to coach Emily to continue to finish her labor. She was having a hard time concentrating on anything but her child. Luckily, her body was doing most of the work automatically.

"Do you want to cut the cord?" Dr. Matthews asked Greg.

Greg looked up bewildered. Dazed love filled his smile and he looked like the happiest deer in the headlights I'd ever seen.

"I guess that was the plan," Greg replied after a moment. He smiled once more at his son before coming around to cut the cord. Dr. Matthews clamped in two places and handed the surgical scissors to the father. Greg cut the cord and then promptly returned to his baby and wife.

I continued to monitor the baby and make sure that Dr. Matthews had the appropriate tools and bins. We were going to have a lot of laundry to do later.

There was a gentle knock on the door and Donna cracked it open, making sure that she still kept the patient's privacy but that we could hear her.

"The chopper just landed," she said through the small crack in the doorway. I hadn't even heard it land. "Everything okay?"

"Excellent," Dr. Matthews replied. The placenta was delivered and Emily's bleeding controlled. He stood up and pulled off his gloves and mask. "And we don't need them. Just a regular ambulance."

"I'll let them know," Donna replied with a grin. "Ambulance will be on it's way to come get him."

"Emily, Greg. The ambulance will take you to the hospital to get checked out," Dr. Matthews informed them. "You don't have to take the helicopter today."

"Okay," Emily said, not looking up at either of us. She was solely and completely focused on her new little baby. As far as she was concerned, he was the only thing in the world that existed.

I couldn't blame her. Newborns had a way of growing on you. They were usually slimy and slippery, but there was something about their little hands that I loved. The way their tiny mouths cried out for someone to care for them always broke my heart. Every time I heard a newborn cry, my maternal instincts seemed to kick in hard.

This time I heard the whirl of the helicopter taking off from the empty field behind us. I'd wondered why it wasn't planted with corn, and now I knew the reason why. It was for helicopters. That made me wonder just how many we called a year.

It wasn't long before the ambulance arrived and we bundled the new little family into the back of the truck. Emily smiled and waved, shouting her thanks to Dr. Matthews, Donna, and me. We stood in front of the office and saw them off.

When the ambulance was safely around the corner, the three of us went back inside the quiet office. I was so incredibly glad that we didn't have more patients. Now that the whole thing was over, I was exhausted and wired at the same time.

"I'll bet that's not what you expected to walk into this

morning, huh?" Dr. Matthews asked with a playful smirk as we walked in.

"Not at all," I admitted. "Look, my hands are shaking."

I held my hands up, watching them tremble.

"It's the adrenaline," he said. "Mine are, too."

Indeed, his hands were quivering just like mine, but with a little less intensity. He took my hands in his and gave them a gentle squeeze. His touch sent electricity up my arms and my core heated.

As if sensing the effect he had on me, he pulled back, his eyes not meeting mine.

"I think we've earned lunch," he said to Donna and I. "My treat. Donna, do we have any more patients scheduled for the day?"

"It's actually ten minutes past closing," Donna informed him. She picked up her purse from under the reception desk. "It's way past lunch."

Dr. Matthews frowned and looked down at his watch. I did the same to see that Donna was right. Time had completely flown by during the delivery. It felt like only seconds.

"Thanks for staying late then, Donna," Dr. Matthews said.

"And miss seeing that baby?" Donna grinned. "I love babies. My babies won't be having their own babies for at least ten more years, so I have to get my baby fix somehow."

I chuckled and waved goodbye to her before going to my office to grab my own purse. It was then that I realized my scrub pants had birth goop on them. When I worked on the Labor and Delivery floor at the hospital, we'd had stacks of backup scrubs in the locker room for just this reason. Births were messy.

Luckily, I always kept a change of clothes in my office. It wasn't anything fancy, just a pair of jeans, sports bra, and a white cotton t-shirt, but it was better than the dirty stuff I had on. After grabbing the clothes, I headed to the office shower.

There was a small shower in the break room near Dr. Matthews' office. It wasn't anything fancy, but it was always nice to have in case we had days like today or needed to rinse a patient off. I grabbed one of the last clean towels from our supply and headed in.

I stripped as I waited for the water to heat, still shaking and grinning with adrenaline. I piled my hair up into a bun to keep it dry. I didn't want to get it wet without shampoo and conditioner.

Everything had gone well. There was a new life in the world and I'd helped get it here. I felt like I could take on the world. There was nothing I couldn't do today.

I sang as I showered, letting myself enjoy the good feelings. Dr. Matthews and I had been an amazing team. I didn't feel hungry or tired anymore. I was pumped. I felt like I could go run a marathon and win. I knew it was all just the excitement and adrenaline from the experience, but I still liked the feeling.

Once clean, I got out and quickly dried off. As soon as I got dressed, I put my hair back into a ponytail and stepped into the hallway. I nearly opened the door right into Dr. Matthews. He jumped back and laughed.

"We've really got to stop doing that," he said. "One of these days, you're going to knock me out with a door."

"Sorry," I said with a smile. "Bad timing, I guess."

My hair was frizzy and I had no makeup on, but Dr. Matthews gave me a slow and obvious once over anyway. It made me feel surprisingly beautiful. When his gaze came back up toward my face, I noticed he stopped for a second too long on my chest. I glanced down, realizing that my nipples had grown hard from the change in temperature and were now poking through my shirt, creating obvious little bumps underneath the cotton. The sports bra was not padded and I hadn't thought it would be a problem.

He cleared his throat and looked into my eyes. "I'm going to take a quick shower, too. Why don't you order some food from the Bakery and have them deliver it here? I'll pay for everything. Get whatever you want. Dessert, drinks, whatever. We earned it."

"Okay, I'll do that," I said, moving out of his way so that he could head into the bathroom. "Meet you in the break room."

## CHAPTER 12

Everything moved slowly in my town. People moved at their own pace here. The bakery said it would be at least an hour before they could have dinner delivered to the office. It wasn't that big of a deal. I was willing to wait for a free meal, and it was still better than a can of soup back at my place. I wasn't ready to go home yet.

There was a soft and comfy couch against the wall in the break room, but I found myself still too pumped up to sit. It was like my body couldn't relax with all the adrenaline that filled it. I paced around for a bit and only stopped when Dr. Matthews stepped into the room.

He'd changed into a casual, lime green polo shirt and gray slacks. His hair was still damp from his shower. He wasn't wearing an undershirt and it was once again apparent how good of shape he was in. The outline of his muscular chest was obvious.

"I needed that," he said, closing the door behind him.

"Me too," I said. "I wanted to tell you that you did great today. Thanks for being awesome. I'm glad you were here."

He took a step toward me, his eyes locking with mine.

84

"Hannah, if it wasn't for you, I couldn't have done any of that."

"I don't know about that." My ponytail swung like a pendulum across my back as I shook my head. "You did all of the hard work."

"Don't sell yourself short," he said assertively, taking another step toward me and closing the gap between us. "I couldn't have done this without you. We were a team. Not to sound too cheesy, but where would Batman be without Robin?"

I laughed. "I think Batman would have been just fine."

"No way," he said. "While Batman was out there taking all the glory, Robin was handling the little things. He was making sure everything went smoothly. You're my Robin."

It was a strange metaphor for our working relationship, but I actually found it endearing and cute. We stood there for a moment, just the two of us, in the privacy of the break room. It was silent except for our breathing and the faint sound of the air conditioner.

Something happened in that moment. I'm not sure exactly what it was, but there was suddenly a magnetic pull that drew me toward Dr. Matthews. It was powerful. So much so, that it felt like even if I had tried to resist it, it wouldn't have made any difference.

He took another small step toward me, bringing the toe of his shoes so that they touched mine. He reached forward and took my hands in his, never taking his eyes off of me for a second.

My heart jumped out of my chest and a burst of energy flowed through me. Dr. Matthews had obviously felt the same pull of attraction that I had. It was electric and so thick in the air that I could practically taste it.

"Hannah," he said softly. "I don't know what I'd do without you."

He lifted one of his hands and brought it to my cheek. His touch caused me to take a quick inward breath. He cradled my chin, lifting it so that our eyes were in direct line of sight. Everything inside of me froze and heated at the same time.

Dr. Matthews leaned in and brought his lips toward mine. He paused right before our lips touched. Just for a moment, though. It was as if he were making sure that I wanted this. The universe held its breath as we both held our breath. I noticed everything from the way his aftershave lingered in the air to the water droplets in his hair. After a second that felt like eternity, he leaned in the rest of the way, firmly pressing his lips against mine.

Our fate was sealed.

A soft moan made its way up my throat as I relaxed into his kiss. I closed my eyes and let my hands drift up toward his face. His beard stubble tickled my fingertips as I dragged them over his cheeks.

It must have been the adrenaline we'd both experienced that morning. Or maybe it was that the emergency had bonded us closer than ever before. I didn't know what had gotten into either of us, but I suppose it didn't need explaining. It felt good and right and that's all I really cared about. I needed a release that only he could give me.

Jacob slowly broke our kiss and dropped his hands to the top of my hips. Then he leaned in again, passionately pressing his lips to mine. My heart began to do flip flops behind my rib cage. Within a few seconds, I felt Jacob open his mouth and gently dart his tongue out, teasing it into my mouth.

A tingling sensation coursed through my body as our tongues lightly wrestled with each others, twisting around in a sensual dance. I reveled in the sensations: his taste, his smell, the way he held his body against mine. This wasn't a dream. This was actually happening.

Jacob broke the kiss and took a step back. His cheeks were flushed and his eyes dark.

"I'm sorry. That was unprofessional."

My heart hammered in my chest and my lips ached for more of his kisses.

"I don't care," I told him. "I don't want to stop."

He looked up, his eyes bright as they met mine. Desire that matched my own shone in them and my body heated. I took the step forward to bring us back together. Slowly, I brought my hand up and wrapped it around the back of his neck.

"Are you sure you're okay with this?" he asked, his hands already coming to my hips.

"Just shut up and kiss me," I said, still smiling.

He kissed me again, only this time it was more passionate, more aggressive. He pulled me close. The warmth of his body radiated against my front, but it was nothing compared to the heat that was building between my legs. Another moan escaped my throat. Our hands drifted up and down each others body and the lust between us soared to an unimaginable height.

*We should try to get emergency calls here more often,* I thought.

It was so amazing that both of us were able to drop our walls and just let go. The way he kissed me showed me that this was something he'd wanted to do for a long time. I guess it just took something drastic for him to realize that the right time is always now.

I took a step back as a concern flashed into my mind. Donna always seemed to forget something and come back to the office most nights. The last thing either of us needed was to be caught making out in there. Something like that would most definitely be the news of the day in a town like ours.

"We should lock the door," I said.

He nodded in agreement and quickly spun around. He turned the lock on the handle and then strolled toward me again. Just like in my dreams, his pupils were dilated as he gave me a once over. There was eagerness in his steps as he closed the gap between us once again.

This time, he didn't stop when his toes met mine. He wrapped his hands around my waist and took a few more steps forward, causing me to back up against the nearby wall. He kept me pressed there, his eyes drifting down toward my chest and then back up. He was breathing harder now. The dam had broken and it was obvious that anything he had held back over the years was finally about to be released.

Something about being backed up against that wall turned me on more than I'd ever been before. I knew that Jacob was powerful, both in work and how he dealt with people. Having that assertiveness focused on me, though, was exhilarating.

As we kissed, I lifted the bottom of his shirt up and placed my hands onto his bare stomach. I could feel his abdominal muscles flex with each of his breaths and I let my fingers trace their way lower, meandering downward toward the top of his slacks.

His hands drifted on my body as well. They started at my hips and then moved their way around. He gently touched the top of my ass and then slid his fingers up my sides, pulling my shirt up along with them. It was now bunched up just below my breasts.

Jacob broke the kiss. I noticed his shoulders moving up and down with his breathing. His eyes had dilated further. It looked like he was a hungry animal about to pounce its prey. I was more than happy to be that prey.

His fingers grabbed the fabric of my shirt and lifted. He dropped the shirt to the floor and stared at me for a moment.

I looked up at him as I pulled the sports bra off and over my head. His eyes dilated.

"Oh, my God," he growled, his voice deep and husky. "You're perfect."

I bit my bottom lip flirtatiously, watching as Jacob admired my body. He seemed so focused on me and only me. It was the same kind of intense focus he had during work. It was like nothing else in the universe existed except me. It made me feel like a princess or a goddess. Something worth worshiping.

He leaned in and brought his mouth over one of my nipples. I drew in a quick breath through my teeth, creating a soft hissing sound. Pleasure washed over me as Jacob flicked the sensitive nub with his tongue, gently lapping at it. Up and down he moved.

He looked up at me without taking his lips away from my breast. He was so damn sexy, just staring up at me with my nipple firmly between his lips. A hint of a smile crossed his face before he focused his attention back on the nipple in his mouth.

Jacob let out a sexual growl and then moved his face to my other breast, giving it equal attention. I closed my eyes and gently pressed the back of my head against the wall. The movement caused my back to arch and my chest to push firmly against his face.

Ecstasy washed over me. I lifted my hands above my head, submitting to him. I wished for him to take me however he wanted. I didn't want to rush anything, though. This was a moment I'd been waiting years for. A moment that I honestly never though would come. Now that it was here, I decided I'd take my time and savor every ounce of it that I could.

I didn't know if I'd ever have this opportunity again. This was spur of the moment. We weren't thinking, we were just feeling. This was the release we both needed. This was biological, not logical. My body overruled my brain, taking control and letting me have what I really wanted.

His hands slid up my sides, to my arms and then to my wrists, pressing my wrists against the wall. Then he broke our kiss once I was pinned.

He leaned forward, his presence overwhelming my senses. His heat pressed against me and all ability to think scattered. He smelled so damn good, like clean soap and fresh air with just a hint of leather.

"I just want to make sure," he said softly, his breath caressing my skin. I shivered with need. There was no way I could say no to him, not with him right there. I'd had a massive crush on him since high school. This was the stuff of dreams.

"Yes," I whispered, my voice full of deep need and years of desire.

I arched my back and kissed him, pressing my hips into his. I could feel him hardening against me, Heat surged between my legs and all I wanted was to have him inside of me. I needed him inside of me.

He released my hands, allowing them to drop by my sides. I then went straight back to undoing the top button of his pants. He stepped back and shrugged out of his shirt, dropping it to the side. I got my first real look at him without clothes on and my imagination wasn't far off.

He was sex on a stick.

"Wow." I didn't even realize I said anything until he smirked. He knew he looked good. With a careless grace, he slid his pants off, kicking them to the side.

I learned then that he was a boxers man. I liked that.

I bit my lip and grinned at him, before pointedly looking at the boxers. "Don't leave a girl wanting more."

"That's the last thing you're going to want," he replied,

hooking his fingers around the waistband and tugging the boxers down slowly. He made sure that I was watching as he inched them down, teasing me with every sexy line of his body. He had the most delicious V that pointed downward to what I really wanted.

He paused with barely a centimeter left before I could see his goods. He stopped and raised his eyebrows, this time giving me the pointed look at my pants. "This isn't a race I'm going to win," he informed me.

I quickly undid the top button of my jeans and shimmied out of them, kicking them to the side where his pants were.

I loved that his breath caught a little at the sight of my lacy panties. They weren't anything special, and so the fact that he reacted that way made me feel sexy as hell. If I had know this was going to happen, I would have worn better ones, but Jacob didn't seem to mind.

Our eyes met and together we removed our underwear at the same time. He was glorious naked. Like an Olympic swimmer mixed with a porn star. All my high school fantasies paled to the reality that was Jacob.

"Wow." This time he was the one who said it. He stared at me like I was the most beautiful thing he'd ever seen. He shook his head in wonder. "Way better than I imagined in high school."

I grinned as he stepped forward and pressed his body against mine, pinning me back against the wall yet again. His skin was hot and I wanted all of it to touch mine. I moaned softly as he kissed my neck, his hands cradling my breasts and his hips rocking in anticipation.

Logic and thought left my head. All that was left was need. I needed to have him inside of me. I needed to feel him more than I needed to breathe. All of the adrenaline from earlier was back, only now it was directed at Jacob.

My legs spread on their own accord. I wrapped one leg

around his waist, opening myself up to him. We both froze for a second as he found my entrance. Our eyes met, and I nodded. He rocked his hip, filling me to the hilt.

He groaned and pressed his head into the curve of my shoulder. I whimpered with pleasure my head falling back against the wall as he completed me in a way I'd never experienced before. This was better than any sex I'd ever had, and we were just at the first stroke.

Together we found our rhythm, rocking our bodies and using the wall as leverage. I wrapped my arms around his broad shoulders, using my leg to keep him wrapped close to me. I loved the way his breath caught at thrust, like each one was better than the one before.

The only thing that existed now was the pleasure he gave me. It became so intense and so focused. It seemed that the only thing I could do was try to remind myself to breathe. My nails dug into his back, yet he kept his relentless pounding. I didn't want him to stop. I never wanted him to stop.

The intensity of it all was dizzying. It was pure euphoria. I rode the wave as far as it would take me and when it peaked, I whimpered my mouth falling open as he pushed me into bliss. My knees buckled and it was only this arms holding me up as I shook against his strength.

I gasped for breath, wanting still more. There was still more for him to give me. He leaned forward and kissed me sweetly, a cocky smile plastered on his face.

"Good?" he asked, already knowing the answer.

I nodded because I couldn't remember how to say yes. He gave me a wicked grin and started the rocking of his hips yet again.

I closed my eyes, losing myself to the sensation. I didn't think. I just felt. I felt his muscles under my fingers. They were strong and lean, his skin hot and damp with sweat. I felt his hips crash into mine, filling me with pleasure in every thrust. I felt his breath on my shoulder, hot and heavy. My own body cried out for more of him. I couldn't get enough.

My entire being was consumed with fire and lust. I craved every inch of his fantastic length and ached to have his skin against mine. His taste drove me wild, his scent made me shiver for him, and the low, masculine groans of his voice created liquid desire deep in my core.

"Hannah," he groaned, his voice tight with need. "Hannah..."

I knew what was about to happen. We hadn't put on a condom, I wasn't on birth control, and I knew there was no way either of us was going to be able to stop.

I didn't care. Now wasn't the time for thinking. Now was the time of doing. I wanted this now more than anything I'd ever wanted in my whole life. It was worth any risk.

"Come for me," I whispered, closing my eyes and pressing my cheek into his.

He exploded, his muscles taut and hard. He shuddered against me, losing himself to me. The man that was so in control at all times lost control in me. The low groan of release as he buried himself and shuddered sent me over the edge. He did it to me without even trying. Together, we found bliss.

Jacob Matthews was mine. For this moment, he was mine. He was the person I'd wanted since I was old enough to want a man. And for this second, I had him. He'd had me since the moment I'd first seen him in that leather jacket walking into to school like he owned the place.

The only sound in the room was the two of us breathing. He panted, his forehead pressed into the curve of my shoulder. My leg still wrapped around his perfect ass and my arms held him tight to me. A sheen of sweat coated both of us.

He kissed my shoulder, his stubble scraping the delicate

skin when he lifted his head. Our eyes met and I lost myself to his baby blues.

I was the luckiest girl in the world.

I unwrapped my leg from around him and we stood toe to toe for a moment. My phone buzzed and I could faintly hear the sound of a car pulling into the clinic's parking lot. Either Donna was back or our food had arrived. My bet was on the food.

He had his hands around the outside of my shoulders and it felt good to be in his arms. It felt safe. He leaned forward and gently kissed my lips. This time, it was more sensual than sexual, and it sent a different kind of tingle through me.

After the delicate kiss, he pulled away, but kept his eyes locked with mine. I felt myself melting into them. Their beautiful light-blue color seemed to ignite as a ray of sunshine from the window poured over them.

He took a step back and I mourned the loss of him. I felt complete with him inside of me, holding me with him. We were two pieces that were made to fit together.

My phone buzzed again and there was the faint sound of a knock on the glass front doors. Our dinner was definitely here.

"I got it." Jacob was already reaching for his pants. He dressed quickly, and unlocked the back room to get our food.

I stared out after him for a moment before scrambling to get my own clothes on. Once dressed, I wasn't sure if I'd just fallen asleep and dreamed what just happened or if my wildest dreams really had come true.

# CHAPTER 13

I sat nervously on the small couch in the break room, my knee bouncing as I tried to figure out what was going to happen next. I was dressed now, and my brain was taking over and rethinking my body's decisions.

I'd just had sex with my boss.

Really, really, *really* hot awesome sex. But with my boss.

I had no idea what Jacob was going to say when he walked back into the break room. Was he going to pretend it didn't happen? Was he going to say it was amazing? Was he going to want to go again?

The uncertainty of it all was killing me.

The door to the break room swung open and my entire body stiffened and turned. I swallowed hard, unsure of what I would say or do next. I wasn't sure what I was going to say to Jacob, but I knew I had to say something.

Until Donna and her two teenage boys walked in. There was no way to have a conversation about anything that just happened with them in the room.

"Donna?" My voice cracked a little with surprise. "What are you and the boys doing here?"

"Danny does the deliveries for the bakery," Donna explained. "I had him move you two up in line to be delivered earlier."

"How very nice of you," I replied. Jacob walked in behind the two teens and Donna and shrugged as I made eye contact with him. He wasn't sure what they were doing here either.

"Alright, I have sandwiches and two of Katie's special brownies." Donna started pulling things out of the bag her tallest son held.

"Mom, I'm supposed to deliver the stuff," the teen told her softly.

"Do you want me to put it back?" she asked, pausing with only one brownie left to go. The poor kid sighed and shook his head. Donna continued setting the food out.

"And I got the spinach salad. Where is it?" Donna mumbled, looking around. "Oh, here it is."

"Are you eating with us?" Dr. Matthews asked. He sounded pleasant but the slight twitch in his eyebrow said he wasn't pleased.

"Just me and Chris," Donna replied, setting out another sandwich. "Danny has more deliveries."

"Oh. That's too bad," I replied automatically. I moved to the table and sat down in front of my food.

"Dr. Matthews, you sit here," Donna instructed, pointing to the seat across from me. "I made sure Katie knew which sandwich was yours so she could pack extra love into it."

Jacob's eye twitched hard. Extra love from Katie wasn't something that needed to be said so soon after what Jacob and I had just done.

"Let's eat." Donna smiled around the table, oblivious to the fact that neither Jacob or I wanted her or her son there.

Conversation was quiet and simple. We made poor Chris talk about school and how his summer was going. He was starting high school in the fall and his voice kept cracking every time he spoke. I swear I've never eaten a sandwich faster than I did for that meal.

All I wanted was to get Jacob alone for a moment so that we could talk about what we'd just done. I knew it was a spur of the moment decision, but I needed to know if it was just an adrenaline release or something more.

I wanted, and yet was terrified, of him saying it was something more.

"That was delicious. Thank you for bringing us dinner," I said, standing up from the table. I'd eaten faster than the teenage boy.

"Oh, my pleasure. You two worked hard today," Donna replied with a smile.

"Dr. Matthews, could I talk to you in my office for a second?" I asked, trying to keep my voice from shaking. "I just wanted to go over some things that happened. You know, for my charting."

"Right. Charting." His blue eyes met mine and he nodded. "Of course."

It was then that my phone chirped. I glanced down at it to see my mother's number, as well as two missed calls from her. Internal alarm bells starting going off. The whole reason I was back in Riversville was to help my father manage his health.

I stopped dead in my tracks. From the corner of my eye I saw Jacob stop moving as well, but I ignored him and read the text from my mother.

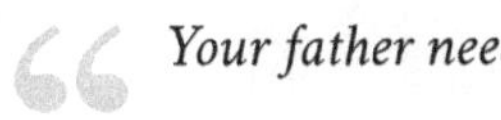

*Your father needs you.*

I thought I was ready to take care of my father. I thought that all my years of nursing would prepare me for this moment, but I wasn't ready. It was my dad. The man I loved all my life. And he needed me.

"Are you okay?" Jacob asked, his brows furrowed.

"My dad needs me," I said, still staring at my phone. I looked up at him and saw concern and understanding in his eyes.

"You should go. We'll go over your charting later," he told me.

"Thanks." I took a step out of the room before remembering my manners. My dad would be angry with me if I didn't have manners because of him. "Thanks for bringing dinner, Donna. And it was good to see you, Chris."

"Bye, Hannah. See you tomorrow," Donna replied, taking a big fork full of salad. I looked back at Jacob one last time and he motioned me to go. I hesitated for just a second before running to my car to get to my father.

# CHAPTER 14

My father was fine.

He and my mother were simply engaged in a discussion on who the actress was on the new TV show they were watching and if she had been on another TV show they also watched.

My father insisted that I would know exactly who they were talking about and that I would prove him right the moment I heard who they were talking about. So, they called me. Repeatedly.

Asking Google or the internet apparently never occurred to them.

After successfully identifying the actress and figuring out that yes, she was on that other show, I went home. I knew Jacob wouldn't stay at the clinic all night waiting for me to come back to discuss our feelings. That didn't stop me from doing a drive-by on my way past, though.

The lights were all off and I felt like an idiot as I sped up and headed the rest of the way back to my house. I justified the drive-by in that it was only four blocks out of my way.

Maybe traffic was backed up by a tractor and I'd actually saved time.

I could pretend that was reasonable.

Once home, I thought of calling Jacob. We needed to have a conversation about what just happened. It had felt so right at the time, but I wasn't sure it was the right thing overall. He was my boss. We weren't supposed to have a sexual relationship.

But I didn't have the guts to call him. I knew he wouldn't call me because he thought I was dealing with a medical emergency for my dad. It was up to me to call him, and I was way too chicken to do it.

Instead, I played Solitaire on my phone trying to work up the courage until I passed out on the couch. I woke up with a crick in my neck and a dead phone. At least the sun woke me, so I wasn't late to work.

However, the entire drive there was torture.

What was I going to say to Jacob? We had sex in the break room, and to be honest, I would never look at that room the same way again. But, he was my friend. And my boss. This was suddenly very awkward and as far from professional as we could get.

Donna was parked in the front, but I didn't see Jacob's motorcycle or his car. I checked my watch to see that I was about ten minutes early, but I had been hoping he'd be early too so that we could talk before patients arrived.

I hoped that he wasn't going to be late just to avoid talking to me.

What if he really regretted what we did? What if he pretended it didn't happen?

I wasn't sure what I would do. I knew that we couldn't date. Not in our town. The town wanted the perfect fairy tale of the good doctor dating the town star baker. They didn't want their most eligible bachelor knocking his boots with the nurse that didn't belong here.

He was the bad boy come home triumphant and I was the girl that left and wasn't staying. If anyone in town thought that the two of us were even thinking of dating one another, I'd be destroyed. He was practically married to Katie in the eyes of the town. I would be the other woman. It wouldn't be pretty.

I swallowed hard before getting out of my car and going inside. I'd actually put on makeup this morning and had attempted to tame my curly hair into something that looked nice. I'd mostly managed to look pretty, and I'd hoped it would give me more confidence that it was. I was a nervous, guilty wreck.

The more I thought about it, the more I realized that what we did was a bad thing. We weren't a couple and we weren't ever going to be. He was my boss. I was leaving in a year or so. I was going to have a major loss in my life. It just wouldn't work out and I should have stopped it before it got this far.

I didn't even want to think about the part of the night where we didn't use a condom. That was stupid. I blamed the adrenaline and the fact that he was so hot I didn't want to stop. It was just one more thing that told me the whole experience, while amazing, was not something we should repeat.

I said hello to Donna and headed to my office to drop off my things. I needed to restock supplies and make sure that the rooms were cleaned up from the night before. I realized I hadn't done any of my usual closing routines and that patients would be here any minute.

I ran to exam room four and threw open the door, expecting to see dried blood and birthing goop. Instead, the room was spotless and everything restocked. I stared at it for a moment before going to the next room to find that it too was cleaned and ready for the day.

I went back to room four just to make sure I wasn't seeing things. Every exam room was clean and ready. Someone had done my job for me last night after I took off to take care of my dad.

"Oh, Dr. Matthews cleaned up last night," Donna informed me, peeking over my shoulder at the clean room. "I can honestly say I've never seen Dr. Taggert do that. This new generation of doctors is something else."

I knew it had nothing to do with what generation of doctors Jacob was part of. It was because of me. He had cleaned up to help me out.

He was too good to be true.

"That Katie sure is a lucky woman," Donna continued. "I heard his mother is planning on performing the ceremony herself. The whole town will be invited."

"What?" I asked, not quite following.

"Dr. Matthews and Katie. You know they're practically engaged, right?"

"Practically isn't actually," I replied. "Why is everyone so dead set on this wedding? I don't even think they're actually a real couple."

Donna raised her eyebrows. "Do you have a problem with Katie?"

"No, I like Katie." I sighed. How could I explain this without giving myself away? "I just haven't seen them as a couple."

"That's just because Katie is so busy," Donna explained. "They make such a perfect couple. It's a fairy tale. He saved her dad, you know. And can you imagine their babies? They'd be so perfect. The entire Bridge Club agrees."

I sighed again. Delusion seemed to be my town's strength. It didn't matter that Jacob and Katie weren't actually a couple. The town, powered by the Ladies' Bridge Club, insisted they were.

Guilt tugged a little bit harder on my soul as I went over the schedule for the day in my office.

If the town found out what happened in that break room, they would hate us. Me especially, but Jacob would lose patients over it. It could damage his business if anyone found out. I didn't want to be the one to bring that to happen.

I heard the front door open and shut. My heart sped up and my palms got sweaty. Jacob was here. The moment I'd been fixated on all night was here. I took a deep breath, smoothed my hair, and raised my chin up. I could do this.

I walked with confidence to the front desk, ready to have a grown up conversation.

Except, Jacob wasn't there. It was Abigail St. James checking in for an appointment.

"Okay, Abigail, you're all checked in," Donna told her. She turned and saw me. "Oh, perfect timing, Hannah. Our first patient is here."

I gave a fake smile. "Of course. Come on back with me."

Abigail audibly rolled her eyes, but came with me.

"Let's get your weight," I said, stopping at the office scale.

"I was just here. I don't need to see those numbers." She crossed her arms and glared at me. "I'm here for a rash, not your sick need to be skinny."

I sighed. "Okay, then. We'll just head to room two."

Once inside, I managed to take her blood pressure and temperature without too much complaint.

"When is Dr. Matthews going to be here?" Abigail asked when I finished.

"Any time now. You're the first patient here, but you did beat him in today."

"Ugh. Figures I'd have to deal with you."

I frowned slightly, unsure of why she was being so hostile

today. I knew she didn't like me and that she hadn't liked me since high school, but usually she at least pretended to be polite.

"Is there something bothering you?" I asked her.

She narrowed her eyes and glared at me.

"I saw you. I saw you with Dr. Matthews and I can't believe that even you would stoop so low."

Panic fluttered in my chest. There was a small window in the break room, but I was fairly sure the blinds were pulled in it. Could she have stopped by the office yesterday and seen us?

"What do you mean?" I asked, deciding to play dumb. Maybe she hadn't seen anything. Maybe I could just say he was checking out a suspicious mole for me. That's why I was naked.

"Don't play dumb," she sneered. "I know you're smart. You should be ashamed of yourself."

"I'm not sure what you saw, but it wasn't what you think," I said slowly. This was not how I wanted the town to find out. Anyone but my high school bully breaking the news would have been preferable.

"I saw you two at the diner. Acting all cozy and friendly." She gave me a dirty look. "He's taken. Even you should be better than that."

"The diner?" I frowned until I remembered that we had gone out to dinner the other night. She hadn't seen us in the break room. "Oh. That was for work."

"Riiiight. 'Work.'" She made the hand motions for quotation marks. "Don't mess with him, Hannah. He's the town hero and you aren't welcome here anymore. The Ladies don't like it when you meddle."

I stared at her for a moment. "I'm not welcome?"

"Nobody wants you back in town, except maybe your parents. We're just fine without you waving your fancy degree around and acting like you're better than us," she told me. "We all know you're just here to get back on your feet. Don't go sticking your nose where it doesn't belong. And it doesn't belong anywhere near Dr. Matthews. You ruin his relationship with Katie, and you'll wish you hadn't."

I stood there in shock for a moment. Abigail was still the queen bee around town and very involved in the Ladies' Bridge Club. If she felt this way, then it was a good bet that most of the other people in town felt the same way. It hurt more than I expected. I'd never been loved by the town, but I'd never been hated either.

A knock on the exam room door took me from my shock and I managed to move out of the way to let Dr. Matthews walk in.

"Good morning, Abigail," he said before realizing I was there. He stopped and stared at me. "Hannah."

He looked so handsome. He had shaved and his dark hair was smoothed back rather than his usual messy. He wore dark blue scrubs that brought out the color of his eyes. The way he looked at me made my stomach do flip flops. I remembered his taste and the way his skin felt pressed against mine.

"Dr. Matthews," I stammered, very aware that Abigail was watching our every move. The last thing I wanted was for her to think there was anything going on. "I was just leaving. All Abigail's vitals look good."

"Good." His eyes met mine and my stomach did the flip-flop thing again.

"Excuse me." I darted out of the exam room as fast as I could. I didn't mean to, but I brushed up against him in the process and the touch sent shivers of want straight through me again. I needed to get a hold of myself.

I closed the door behind me, hearing Dr. Matthews start talking to Abigail through the wooden door.

"Dr. Matthews, it's so good to see you. How are you and Katie doing?" Abigail asked sweetly. "I hear you'll have a ring for her soon."

"Katie and I aren't a couple," he said gently.

"If you say so, Dr. Matthews. You two have been so discreet and proper. There's not many in town that would take their time and really make sure things are going to work the way you two have."

Dr. Matthews sighed. "We aren't a couple," he repeated and I could hear it in his voice that he was tired of saying it and not having anyone listen. "Now, let me see how the rash is doing."

I stepped away from the door. I had work to do and I didn't need to eavesdrop on Abigail's appointment. I could already hear from the gentle hum of voices in the waiting area that we were filling up with patients. It sounded like it was going to be another busy day.

I didn't get a chance to say anything to Dr. Matthews all morning. We kept running into one another in our work duties, and we talked about patients and vitals and medications, but there was always either a patient or Donna around listening.

I suddenly understood why those cheesy romance novels my mom liked to read were always talking about "meaningful glances." It was exactly what Jacob and I did all day. Our eyes tried to have a conversation that our words couldn't.

"Let me walk you out, Mrs. Johnson," I said to my last patient before lunch. It looked like we might actually have a break.

"You are too sweet," the elderly woman said, patting my hand as she stood up. "I wasn't sure how well you'd do back in Riversville, but you sure brought some professionalism with you."

"Um, thank you?" I wasn't quite sure what she meant by that, but since Mrs. Johnson was the preacher's mother and one of the main organizers of the Bridge Club games, I was glad she wasn't talking to me like Abigail had earlier.

"It's refreshing to see young people take the time to have manners," Mrs. Johnson explained. "You need to find a good man and have some babies. I heard that Dan Marston is single. He and his wife just divorced last year. He's a nice man. Unfortunately, I think he's the only single man in town at the moment."

"Really?"

"Well, there's Samuel. But he's a bit older than you." Mrs. Johnson thought for a moment. "Who else is there? Dr. Matthews is marrying Katie, Jameson Richards is taking out Jane Andres, Jim Sands is a drunk and you don't want him, and Paul Dunes is gay. I'm afraid the selection is rather poor at the moment."

I sighed.

"Don't worry, though," Mrs. Johnson continued. "I'm sure you'll find someone. You're still young enough to have at least one baby. I wouldn't worry. At the next bridge game, we'll think of someone for you. You deserve to have some happiness."

"That's very kind of you." I cringed inwardly at the idea of my love life being the topic of conversation at the next ladies bridge game. The games were invite only and where most of the town gossip and decisions were made. It was like a mafia meeting, if mafiosos were small-town women with too much time on their hands.

I think I would have preferred the mob, to be honest.

"You have a wonderful afternoon, Mrs. Johnson." I held open the clinic door for her. She smiled at me.

"We'll find you someone even if we have to get you a date from Des Moines," she told me.

I did my best to smile until she was out of sight.

"You better be careful if the Ladies are figuring out your love life," Donna said from her desk. "I'll try to stick up for you, but I can't guarantee they won't decide you need to marry Dan in the next three weeks."

"Thanks, Donna." I shook my head. I would not be swayed by whatever the Ladies decided. "Any more news about the lunch?"

"Just a little bit," Donna replied. "And Dr. Taggert brought lunch. There's pizza in the break room."

"Really?" I asked surprised. I had planned on a boring sandwich from home. Pizza was way better. Especially free pizza.

"He heard about the birth last night and wanted to congratulate us." Donna took a big bite of pizza at her desk. "Go get some."

I grinned and hurried to the break room to find Dr. Matthews and Dr. Taggert sitting at the break room table eating pizza together. I had to consciously force myself not to look at the wall where Jacob had pressed me up and made me shiver with pleasure. As if sensing my thoughts, Dr. Matthews looked up at me.

"Hannah." The sound of his voice saying my name gave me goosebumps.

Dr. Taggert turned and grinned at me. He usually played Santa for all the kids at Christmas, and even in the summer he still had the white beard, though he kept it trimmed short. "Hannah!"

The difference in reaction to the two men saying my name only underlined how I felt about Dr. Matthews. He gave me the tingles while Dr. Taggert seemed like he was simply making sound.

Dr. Taggert stood up and shook my hand. "Jacob here was

telling me how instrumental you were last night. He says he couldn't have done it without you."

"Thank you," I replied, not looking at Jacob. "I could have done it without him."

"I miss having a nurse like you," he  "Come have a seat and eat some pizz

I smiled and followed him to th Jacob. Yet again, we were unable we needed to. My heart thumy time Jacob even glanced in my direc

"Hannah? We have a walk, Donna said, poking her head into the break room. "It's just a suspected strep throat."

"I got it," Dr. Matthews said, standing up quickly. "You eat."

He gave me a quick smile and another one of those meaningful glances. I nodded.

"He's a good doctor," Dr. Taggert observed as Jacob left the room. "I'm glad I picked him to take over the practice. He's doing better than I could have hoped."

I nodded and reached for a piece of pizza. My stomach rumbled as the scent of cheese hit me.

"Did you have other people that wanted the practice?" I asked, taking a big bite.

"Two actually," Dr. Taggert replied. "They were both from out of town, so someone native to Riversville was my preference. I wasn't sure, given Jacob's admittedly spotty history, but he's proven himself."

I nodded and swallowed. "He's a different person than he was as a teenager. He's grown up a lot."

"That he has. I almost regret giving him the morality clause in his contract." Dr. Taggert paused and then picked up another slice of pizza. "He's proving that he didn't even need it with how well he's been running the clinic."

"Morality clause?" I swallowed down a big bite of pizza.

Dr. Taggert shrugged. "I thought it prudent given his bad-boy ways. Without going into detail, he has to maintain appropriate relationships in the community. You know, no scandals. This is a business that I built from the ground up and I don't want it to fall to pieces because the man I sold it to can't keep it in his pants."

I choked a little on my pizza and started to cough.

"Are you okay?" Dr. Taggert asked, concern filling his features.

"I'm fine," I managed to get out. "Just swallowed funny."

He watched me for a second before taking my word for it. "Anyway, I know that he's not really seeing Katie, but he's sure been a good sport. He knows that the Ladies' Bridge Club is the way to the town's heart. I'm glad he's got a good head on his shoulders. Upsetting them would not be good for the business."

"And the business is still yours?" I asked, hoping I didn't sound like I was prying.

"It is. I was worried about giving up the practice, but Jacob is putting my mind at ease. A few more years of him running the clinic and keeping a low profile, and I'll be more than happy to finalize everything. I might even be ready to retire by then."

He chuckled.

"So, you still own the practice? If Dr. Matthews screws up he won't be able to buy it?" I asked, feeling my heart sink.

"Yes. If Jacob does anything that damages the image of the practice, I won't sell it to him. I don't see him doing that, though." Dr. Taggert took a bite of his pizza. "He's not the hot-headed kid he used to be. He makes good decisions now."

I nodded and set my pizza down. I wasn't hungry any more. In fact, I felt a little sick to my stomach.

"Feel free to have another slice," Dr. Taggert said, motioning to the box. "I got us plenty."

"I'm full," I replied. "I actually need to finish some charting. It was good to see you, Dr. Taggert. Thank you for the pizza."

I headed out of the break room and went to my office and closed the door. Guilt weighed heavier on my shoulders with every step.

If word got out that Dr. Matthews and I had banged in the break room, the Bridge Club would be furious. They would ruin Dr. Matthews' reputation, which would hurt the practice. Given the morality clause that I'd just learned about, that meant that Jacob would lose the practice.

I couldn't do that to him. He loved this practice and the town. I was only going to be here for a year or two. It wasn't fair to ask him to risk everything to be with me when I couldn't even say for sure that I would be here in a year.

I had to give him up. No more break room encounters. We would be professionals. What happened yesterday had to be a one time thing. I was going to resist those blue eyes and perfect ass. I told myself it wouldn't be hard, even though I knew that was a lie.

I slumped into my desk chair. Between Abigail's threats and Dr. Taggert's clause, this day sucked.

A soft knock caught my attention. "Come in," I said, straightening up in my chair. It was probably Donna coming to tell me we had patients.

Instead, Jacob opened the door. Despite my decision not to be attracted to him, my heart still sped up. I couldn't help but notice the smooth motion of his muscles under his scrubs and the way the light caressed his hair.

He closed the door behind him.

"Hi."

"Hi." I swallowed hard. "We need to talk."

He nodded, but before he could say something that would make me change my mind, I spoke first.

"Yesterday was a mistake," I told him, watching his face to see his reaction. His eyes widened, but he didn't look too surprised. "We can't do it again."

"I agree," he said softly. "It was the adrenaline and the situation. We weren't thinking clearly."

I hated hearing him say it. I had this secret hope that he was going to tell me that he actually loved me and that it wasn't a mistake.

But that was something for rom-com movies and daydreams.

"We're still friends, though, right?" I asked, my heart in my throat. I liked spending time with him and the other night at the diner, with absolutely no romantic intentions, had been amazing. I didn't want to lose that.

Jacob's face softened and his shoulders dropped. "Of course we're still friends. We never stopped."

That made me feel at least a little bit better.

"Okay. Then we just pretend that nothing happened last night." I wanted to add on "even though you were amazing," but that didn't feel like it would help the situation. We were trying to move away from having sex, and telling him he was a sex god wouldn't help with that.

"Exactly." Jacob nodded, his eyes meeting mine and I swear I saw the same heat as the night before.

We stood there for a moment, just looking at one another and not saying how attractive the other person was. Luckily, there was a knock on my door before Donna poked her head in.

"Patients are here," she announced. She frowned and looked at the two of us. "What's up with you two and the long faces? You've both been weird all day."

"It's, uh..." Jacob stammered for a reason.

"Babies," I stepped in, standing up from my chair.

"Oh, Well, the full moon is over and we don't have any super pregnant women as patients currently," Donna replied. "No more surprise babies for you two." She narrowed her eyes and looked at me. "Unless you've been having extra curricular activities."

"What? Me?" I felt my cheeks turn bright red. Did Donna know?

"I'm just messing with you," she told me with a chuckle. "You are so serious sometimes." She shook her head as she walked down the hallway.

I looked up at Dr. Matthews. For some strange reason, I didn't want this moment to end. I didn't want to be apart from him, even if it meant we were just standing in my office staring at each other.

"You two coming or what?" Donna called from the hallway. "We have folks to see."

Jacob and I looked at each other one more time before he turned and left my office. I let out a slow breath, unsure of how I felt about things.

It wasn't going to happen again. It was a one time thing. We were just friends and coworkers.

Yet, somehow, I found myself hating that and wanting so much more.

# CHAPTER 15

*I* left work that day with a conflicted heart. Dr. Matthews and I worked well the rest of the day. We'd joked with patients and were even alone in the break room for a whole five minutes without taking our clothes off.

We could do this, I told myself. It would get easier with time. Maybe by next week I wouldn't want to jump his bones every time I saw him. Maybe by next month, I would forget just how good he felt inside of me. How I had felt complete.

Maybe.

But probably not.

I sighed as I put my car away and headed into the house. A summer storm chased the setting sun across the corn fields. Big, heavy, gray clouds filled the darkening sky and thunder rumbled as I went inside. The smell of rain on growing things and the cool breeze of a storm filled my home.

The humidity still flowed around me like water, but the storm would at least lower the temperature to something almost comfortable. I thought a quick shower and then I would sit by my window and watch the rain come in.

I ran upstairs and started the water. I tried not to think of Jacob as I undressed. I tried not to think of him as I washed my hair. I tried not to think of how he would like my legs smooth as I shaved them. I tried not to think of the way his hands felt on my hips, the strength of his fingers against my skin, the taste of his lips and the heat of his body.

I failed at not thinking of him.

I put on a pair of comfy cotton shorts and a cute t-shirt. Rain pattered on the windows and thunder rumbled overhead. My air conditioner kicked on and for the first time in weeks, I actually felt a little cool.

I went to the kitchen and started to make some dinner. I had some chicken breasts and local sweet corn and veggies. It wasn't going to be fancy, but it would taste good and make great leftovers for tomorrow. One of the perks of living in a farming town was that we had the best produce at the farmer's markets.

I started prepping the corn, trying not to think of Jacob and the way his muscles flexed. I decided I would watch TV with dinner tonight, or I'd spend my entire meal trying not to think of him and how we weren't going to be together ever again.

My doorbell rang. I paused with the corn half stripped and frowned. A flash of lightning lit the sky and rain pelted the roof. It was not the time of day to be outside.

I hurried over to the door and threw it open. Standing on my porch, soaking wet and looking hotter than hell, was Jacob Matthews.

His bike sat under my garage awning and he had his helmet in his hands. His hair was the only dry thing on him from being under his helmet. I tried not to stare at the way the water ran off his leather jacket or the fact that his jeans were totally soaked and sticking to his skin.

"Come in," I said, throwing the door open. "What are you doing out here in the rain?"

He stepped inside and carefully set his helmet on the entryway floor. I took his jacket and hung it on my coat tree. His light blue t-shirt was splattered with water, highlighting the curves of his muscular chest. It was hard not to stare and lick my lips at the same time.

He ran a hand through his hair, making it stand up. "I didn't like the way we left things at the office today," he explained.

I frowned. We'd both said a polite goodbye and left. He went on his bike, I'd gotten in my car, and Donna had waved to both of us.

"Okay." I nodded like that made sense. "Let me grab you a towel."

It was as good an excuse as any to give me a moment to compose myself. Jacob Matthews, the sexiest man alive, was soaking wet and at my house. This was a temptation that I wasn't sure I could handle. I hoped he was a stronger person than I was.

I came back with a towel to find that he'd stripped off his wet shirt. Instead of just standing wet in my house, he was now wet and half-naked in my house.

I handed him the towel, trying not to stare at his skin. "You said you wanted to talk?"

He nodded. "I went home and I realized that we didn't go over everything."

I nodded. I couldn't help it, but I was turned on. It was taking all my will power not to reach out and touch him. My fingers knew how good his skin would feel.

"Right. You're here to talk."

I quivered with desire as he took a step toward me. Our

eyes met and we both knew that he wasn't here to have a conversation.

Our bodies flew into a kiss as if we were magnets. Our lips collided, his arms tangling into my hair as he pressed himself to me. All the energy spent trying to stay apart changed into trying to get closer together.

My fingers reached for his pant buttons as he pulled my shirt up and over my head.

"I wanted to talk to you about work," he said, stepping out of his pants once I'd released the button. He shimmied out of his briefs, leaving him gloriously naked other than his wet socks.

He tossed my shirt to the side and tugged at my shorts. I moved my hands to take over, doing quick work of taking everything off.

"We really should be more professional," I gasped as he bent his head and took my nipple into his mouth.

"Professional is a good word," he murmured against my breast before flicking his tongue against me. I moaned, taking his head into my hands. His hair was warm between my fingers.

"We should probably sit down to discuss this," I gasped, arching my back into him. His mouth was magic against me.

"You're absolutely right," he agreed. He stood up and glanced around before seeing my couch. He reached down and grabbed a condom out of his jeans pocket and then met me by the couch.

"Have a seat," I told him, pushing gently on his shoulder. He sat, and I straddled his lap. He was already hard and ready to go against me. I rocked against him, not taking him in yet. The heat in my core shot up two levels knowing that he wanted me.

"We should discuss proper workplace decorum," he thrust upward, seeking the source.

"You're absolutely right," I whimpered, taking the condom from him. "I think we can keep things professional in the office. It's very doable."

"I'm so glad you agree," he groaned as I slid the condom down over him. He felt so good in my hands, I couldn't wait to feel how good he would feel in other places.

"I'm glad we had this chat," I told him, raising myself up and over him. Our eyes met. His eyes were dark and heated. His hair was messy from my fingers. Lightning flashed but I couldn't hear the thunder over the sound of my pounding heart.

"I think we've come to an excellent agreement," he agreed before thrusting into me.

Bliss washed through me as I threw my head back and savored the feeling of him.

He rocked his hips in time with mine, the lighting flashing and thunder masking all the sounds of our bodies joining.

His mouth kissed along my shoulder and throat, up to my mouth. I kissed him. I'd wanted to kiss him since the moment I knew him. I'd wanted to kiss him every moment we'd spent together today. It had nearly killed me to know I would never know his taste again.

So I relished this. I took my time and kissed him. I felt every inch of his skin, my hands ran along his shoulders and back as I rode him. Thunder rumbled outside, but it was nothing compared to the electricity flowing between the two of us as we fucked.

We panted with need, each of us pushing the other to go faster and harder. Need drove us. This wasn't slow and sensual. This was instinctual and hard. We needed to feel one another. We needed to find our release so that we could then go slow and steady.

I melted into him as he moved inside of me, rubbing up

against him, making him groan. His skin stuck to mine with the humidity and our sweat. I wanted more of him. I wanted all of him. His hand went to my front, fingers splayed on my hip and his thumb strumming my clit like a guitar.

I could feel the controlled strength in his every movement. He was stronger than me, but using his strength only to make my world pleasurable. His thumb swirled a delicious pattern, ratcheting up the intensity of pleasure with every circle.

"Jacob..." I whispered, finding myself cresting a wave of his making. Everything about him caused sensations in my body that I didn't even know what to do with. My legs squeezed around his waist, my arms around his shoulders.

"Come for me," he commanded, his voice firm. I lost myself to him, doing exactly as he asked. There was no fear or shame, just desire and a willingness to please. My body tensed and relaxed at the same time, finding a blinding bliss.

"You are so hot when you let go," he growled, his core shaking against mine. With a groan, he dropped his head to the curve of my shoulder and gently bit down. He tensed, a whimper leaving his body as he too found release and lost himself to me.

The idea that I could do that to him, that my orgasm could cause his was enough to send me over the edge again with him. Together, we cried out, losing control in the best possible way. We were tangled and sweaty, but together.

Panting, slowly we came back to our senses. Other than our breathing, the rain was the only sound.

I slid to the side and he cuddled me into him, our bodies hot and sticky next to one another. I didn't want to move away from him. I could still feel the after effects of the pleasure he'd just given me. It was like being drunk but without the hangover. I felt amazing.

"We suck at not having sex," I said once I could breathe normally.

"And we did so well for so long," Jacob commented. "We went years without having sex. Now we can barely go twenty-four hours."

I giggled, nestling my head onto his shoulder. He smoothed my hair and sighed with contentment.

"What are we going to do?" I asked softly, half afraid he would tell me yet again that this was a mistake.

"I don't want to give you up," he replied, his hand still smoothing my hair. "I don't think I can now."

I couldn't help the smile that filled my face. I sat up so I could see him. "Then don't."

He grinned at me. "Okay."

I smiled and snuggled back into him, his arms wrapping around me and keeping me close. For this moment in time, we could pretend it was that simple.

"Thank you, Hannah," Dr. Matthews said, handing me a patient chart as I passed his office.

"Of course, Dr. Matthews," I replied sweetly. I smiled at him, but it was a professional smile. One I would give any coworker.

We'd managed to go the entire rest of the week without having sex in the office.

But that was only because we were having lots of sex in other places. My bed. His bed. My kitchen. His living room.

So far, no one suspected a thing. Not even Donna. We were the models of professionalism and good behavior at work. Other than a couple of winks here and there. It took a lot for me not to smack his perfect ass when he walked past, but I was capable of controlling myself

Especially because I knew that it meant I got to have him all to myself later.

"What are you up to tonight?" he asked, swiveling in his chair.

"Just a quiet night in," I told him. "My place. All alone."

Which meant that I wanted him to come to my place.

He grinned. "Sounds like a nice relaxing night. I was thinking of cooking tonight, myself. I have some salmon I need to eat."

Which meant that he wanted me to come over to his house for more than just salmon.

"Sounds delicious," I told him with a smile. "Enjoy your dinner."

Which meant I would be at his house after work.

I flashed him one more smile before taking the file to Donna's front desk. I tucked it into the pile of to-be filed charts. Despite having a paperless system in place, we still used a lot of paper.

"Hey, Hannah," Karina greeted me, worry in her voice. She stood on the opposite side of Donna's desk. Leigh Ann held her hand and looked pale.

"Hey!" I smiled at her and then frowned at Leigh Ann. "Why are you guys here?"

"I don't feel good," Leigh Ann announced.

And then promptly vomited all over the floor.

Karina stared at her daughter in shock. "I didn't think she had any more left in her," she said softly.

I hurried around the desk to get to Leigh Ann. She sniffled and wiped at her face, looking utterly dejected.

"Let's get you in a room and cleaned up," I told her, gently taking her arm.

"I'll clean this up," Karina announced, but didn't move an inch. She looked like she might throw up too. Karina wasn't good with bodily fluids.

"I've got it," Donna told her. "You wouldn't believe how often this happens. That's why Dr. Taggert had the tile installed a few years ago. I broke the carpet cleaner and tile was the cheaper option."

Donna reached into her magic desk and pulled out a roll of paper towels and a bottle of spray bleach. I had no idea where she kept most of the supplies under there. She snagged a pair of gloves from a box of them on the counter and quickly went to work cleaning everything up. There was less on the floor than it had originally sounded like.

"You come with me," I told Leigh Ann with a smile, and I carefully took her to one of the exam rooms.

"She's been feeling unwell all day," Karina explained, still looking a little pale herself. "I thought she just had a stomach bug, but she's got a fever and she says her stomach hurts."

"You were good to bring her in," I told her. I carefully took Leigh Ann's temperature and found that it was well over one-hundred. "Have you given her any medicine?"

"Some Tylenol about two hours ago," Karina replied. She chewed on her bottom lip, worry for her child painting her face. "You know I don't do the sick thing. I brought her in when she still said it hurt."

"Okay." I motioned to Leigh Ann to get up on the exam table. I noticed that she grimaced a little bit with the motion and I started to worry. "Leigh Ann, can you show me where it hurts?"

Leigh Ann pointed to the right side of her stomach.

"I'm going to feel around on your belly," I told her. "If it hurts, I want you to let me know." I gently pushed on her upper belly and Leigh Ann shook her head. I could feel the heat of her skin through my gloves.

"Ouch," she whimpered when I touched her lower stomach.

"Does it hurt more when I push in, or let out?" I asked, doing the motion as gently as possible.

"Out." Leigh Ann's lower lip trembled.

"You're very brave, Leigh Ann." I knew what this was. Appendicitis. "I'm going to go get Dr. Matthews. You're both doing great."

Karina went and held her daughters hand. Leigh Ann

leaned into her mother and I could see her relax at her mother's touch. Even though I was her friend, I wasn't her mother. A part of me ached to feel that bond.

I hurried out of the room and found Dr. Matthews at his desk. I knocked on his door and was greeted with a megawatt smile when he saw who it was.

"Hi," he greeted me. "Just thinking about my salmon later."

I smiled and then quickly shook my head. This wasn't the time for secret fish meeting discussions.

"Leigh Ann has appendicitis," I told him. "I'll call St. Joe's and tell them to expect her."

"You're sure?" he asked, his face suddenly serious.

"Rebound tenderness in the lower right quadrant, fever, and vomiting."

He nodded. "I'll go talk to her mom."

He stood up as I went to my office and called the hospital. They would have a surgical consult ready for Leigh Ann when she arrived.

"Hannah, we need your help. Leigh Ann's mom is freaking out," Donna said, coming into my office.

I frowned, unsure of what Donna was talking about until I got to the hallway. Karina was sitting in one of the patients chairs and crying. Leigh Ann sat in her lap looking confused.

"What do I do? I don't know what to do," she mumbled, rocking back and forth. She wasn't moving to get in the car and Donna looked frustrated.

"I don't think she's safe to drive," Donna said to no one in particular.

"How many more patients do we have today?" Dr. Matthews asked Donna.

"Just two," Donna replied without even having to check the schedule.

"Okay. I think we can handle that on our own." Dr.

Matthews put his hand on my shoulder and it took all my willpower not to show how much I enjoyed it. "Will you drive them to St. Joe's? She's not going to be able to do it."

I didn't have to think twice about that. I was Leigh Ann's godmother. If I had to carry her there on my back I would do it.

"Of course." I nodded and then realized that it would be a while at the hospital tonight. "I guess my quiet night in isn't happening."

He nodded, understanding my code. I wouldn't make dinner tonight. "I'm sure you might be able to have one later."

He would wait up for me.

I flashed him a small smile before going to Karina and Leigh Ann. "Come on, Karina. Let's go get in the car. I'll drive."

She sputtered a thank you as she clung to her daughter. It took a moment for her to realize that we were leaving. She grabbed her things and then handed me her keys.

"You drive. I'm not good," she told me. I smiled and nodded. Karina was an awesome friend, but she tended to freak out in emergencies.

We got Leigh Ann in the car and Karina sat in the backseat so she could hold her daughter's hand for the drive. It took me a moment to figure out all the controls for the minivan, but we were off in no time.

The drive to the hospital was uneventful. Karina sat in the backseat looking like she was headed to a funeral and Leigh Ann slept. I tried to tell her that this was a common thing, but Karina was too wrapped up in her worry to really listen. I put on some of her favorite music and and just drove.

At the hospital, things went to plan. The surgical consult agreed that it was appendicitis and Leigh Ann was whisked off to surgery. I sat with Karina and kept her calm while they operated on her daughter.

Karina's husband, Tom, showed up, looking far calmer than Karina.

"Is she okay?" he asked me, giving his wife a hug.

"She's in surgery," I told him. "They should be done soon."

"Thanks for being here." Tom squeezed his wife. "I knew she'd be okay with you, Hannah."

I smiled at the compliment. We all stood when a surgeon came out a few minutes later. Karina clung to Tom.

"She did great," the doctor announced. "We caught it with plenty of time. She'll be in recovery for a little while, and then you guys can head home."

"Oh thank god," Karina gasped, collapsing into a chair. Relief rippled out of her in waves. I couldn't blame her. I had been worried about Leigh Ann, too, but I knew what was going on. Still, it was a relief to know my favorite kid was okay.

"Can we go back and see her?" Tom asked the doctor.

"Sure. I can bring two of you back," he replied.

"I'm going," Karina said, getting to her feet. "She needs me."

Tom glanced over at me.

"I'll head home," I told him. "She's safe and in good hands. If you need anything tonight, you have my number."

Gratitude washed over his face. "You should take my truck," he said, handing me the keys. "We'll drive the van home."

I took the keys from him and gave them both hugs. "Give Leigh Ann all my love, and tell her I'll see her right away," I told them. They both promised to give her hugs and kisses just for me.

I watched as they held one another and headed back to the post-surgery area. My heart ached. As much as I loved Leigh Ann, she wasn't my daughter. I wasn't going to go back to her and make her smile. I wouldn't be the person she wanted to see.

I sighed and pocketed the keys. Just then my phone buzzed. It was Jacob with a picture of salmon on the grill.

*All yours if you're hungry,* said the message.

I smiled, feeling my spirits lift. Leigh Ann was safe and I was going to see a handsome man and get dinner. Life wasn't so bad.

I headed out to the parking lot only to realize I hadn't asked Tom where he parked. I pulled out the keys and started hitting buttons. I was going to have to play the "where's my truck" game in the parking lot. I just hoped that Tom parked close.

# CHAPTER 17

It took me ten minutes to find Tom's truck. Luckily, security didn't bother me since it was still mostly daylight out and I was obviously looking for a car. I imagined that this happened fairly frequently.

I thought of seeing Jacob and my body went hot and fuzzy at the thought. I took off my scrub top to show off the low cut tank top I wore underneath. I had made sure to wear my sexy bra today. With the way Jacob and I were going, it was a good idea to wear a sexy bra everyday.

Tom's work truck chugged down the highway as I made my way back home. Twilight crept along the road behind me, finally overtaking me with darkness a few miles from town. I sung along to the radio as I turned down the street leading to Jacob's house. I was going to have to tell Jacob that he needed more light on his street. It seemed like none of the street-lights were bright enough.

That's when I saw the police cruiser flip a u-turn and put on its lights behind me.

I mumbled a curse and pulled to the side of the road. My heart started pounding. I'd been pulled over a grand total of two times in my entire life. This would be the third, and I had no idea where the registration or proof of insurance was for the car.

I turned off the engine and kept my hands on the steering wheel. It wasn't because that was what I was supposed to do. It was because my hands were shaking too badly to put them anywhere else.

A flashlight tapped on my window and it took me a moment to find the right buttons to make the window lower.

"Evening, Officer." My voice cracked. "Is there a problem?"

"Is that you, Hannah?" A light shone in my face and I squinted for a moment until it moved. "It is you."

"Oh. Hello, Officer Matthews," I stammered. I probably should have called him Chief Matthews, but I wasn't sure what his real job title was. He was Jacob's father. He was also the chief of police for Riversville, but I had known him as Officer Matthews growing up.

Officer Matthews frowned slightly at me. The two men were of a similar build, but Jacob had more of his mother's lean lines. Mr. Matthews had a stronger chin and darker hair, but the same blue eyes as his son.

"What are you doing driving the Rochesters' truck?" Officer Matthews asked. He ran his flashlight over the length of the vehicle.

"Leigh Ann, their daughter, had to go to the hospital. I drove her and her mother in their car," I explained. "Tom told me to take his truck home since I didn't have a car."

Officer Matthews nodded. He put the flashlight away. "Do you know why I pulled you over?"

I did a quick mental check and couldn't remember how fast I was going. It didn't feel fast in the big truck, but that didn't mean I wasn't speeding. "I, uh.... I mean, uh..."

"Your headlights aren't on," Officer Matthews supplied.

I smacked my head with my hand. They weren't automatic on the truck. No wonder it felt so dark. I couldn't see not because the street lights were dim, but because I was.

Officer Matthews chuckled. "What are you doing on this side of town anyway?" he asked. "The only person that lives out here is Jacob. Why are you going to see him at this time of night? I was just coming from his place. I half expected to see Katie out here, not you."

My skin went cold. I couldn't tell him that I was off to shag his son. Especially since he seemed to be under the impression Jacob was with Katie.

That would not go over well. I remembered Officer Matthews as being more patient than his wife, but it still wasn't something I was excited to share. I tried to resist the urge to tug on the straps of my tank top and hide the cleavage spilling out of my shirt. I knew the lace was poking out and it was all I could do not to bring attention to it.

"Oh, you must be giving Jacob an update. He worries about his patients," Officer Matthews said, saving me from coming up with a lie myself.

"Yup. That's it."

"You could have just called," he remarked, giving me a sidelong look.

"Yes. I could have, but this is on my way home. That way I don't have to drive and talk on the phone or make him wait to get the updates," I replied. It sounded ridiculous even as I said it, but I smiled and hoped it sounded believable. "Also, it's important for medical reasons."

"Then I won't keep you," Officer Matthews replied. He gave me a serious frown. "Turn on your headlights. You get a warning this time since it isn't your truck."

"Thank you, Officer Matthews."

He tipped his hat and walked back to his cruiser. My

hands were shaking so badly I was afraid to drive. I did manage to find the headlights and turn them on.

Officer Matthews blipped his lights at me and left me hyperventilating on Jacob's street. This was a close call. Super close. My boobs were nearly falling out of my tank top and I'd barely managed to say why I was driving to Jacob's house.

Only when the police cruiser was completely out of sight did I have the courage to start the engine and finish the drive to Jacob's house. He lived in a cute little house on the end of a long dirt road. It had been in his family for generations, much as my house was in mine.

I pulled up to the front door and glanced around before getting out. When the porch light flicked on, I half expected his mother to come walking out. At least this time I had my scrub top back on and looked half way respectable.

Jacob opened the door as I walked up the wooden steps.

"Hey there," he said softly, reaching out to kiss me. I took a step back and then darted into his house. Confusion crossed his face as he followed, shutting the summer night out behind us. The air conditioner hummed in the window. "What's up?"

I locked the door and then kissed him. He tasted like cold beer and apple pie.

"You okay?" he asked when I broke the kiss and leaned against him.

"Your dad pulled me over," I told him. "On the dirt road."

I felt him tense underneath me. This was the only house out here. It was pretty damn obvious where I was going if he pulled me over on this road. "He just showed up earlier. Walked right in. What did he say?"

"He thinks I'm giving you a report on how things went at the hospital," I told him. "They went great by the way. No issues."

Jacob let out a slow breath, his hands making slow circles on my back.

We both knew how close we came to getting caught. If his dad had come over while I was here, I wouldn't have an excuse. Especially if he walked in on us doing the horizontal tango. I was sure Officer Matthews wouldn't be pleased to find me under his "practically engaged" son.

I really wished that rumor would die.

"Remind me to start locking the door," Jacob said after a moment. Apparently we were both thinking the same thing. I wasn't sure that the locks even worked on either of our doors given that no one in town locked their doors ever, but at least it would give us time if someone came over unannounced.

We would just have to say that it was a habit we picked up in the city.

I hated that I was coming up with preemptive lies. I wished that we could just date like normal people, but Jacob was my boss. He was also my boss that most of the town thought should marry someone else regardless of how he felt about it.

"You want some dinner?" Jacob asked. "I bet you're hungry."

My stomach rumbled as if on cue. "That would be great."

He gave me an extra squeeze before letting me go and guiding me to the kitchen. He had grilled a large piece of salmon and lots of veggies. It smelled delicious.

"What'd you tell your dad about all the food?" I asked, getting a plate from the cabinet.

"I'm meal prepping. Left overs are easier on my schedule," Jacob replied with a shrug. He took out a cup and poured me a whiskey. "And it's true. I don't think you're eating five pounds of salmon."

"I don't know, I'm awfully hungry," I teased, putting a big chunk of fish on my plate.

"If you eat it all, I will be super impressed. Not even mad, just impressed."

I grinned and speared a bite with my fork. It was perfect. Flaky and soft with a smoky flavor from the grill. "This is fantastic. Thank you."

We sat at his kitchen table as I wolfed down probably close to a third of his delicious salmon. I didn't eat all of it, but it was close. Combined with the whiskey, I finally started to relax.

Still, every time I thought I heard a car outside, I froze.

"Do we have a game plan?" I asked after jumping at the air conditioner starting for the third time. "Is this how it's always going to be?"

"No. I talked to Katie yesterday. We're going to have a nasty breakup when she gets back from filming her cooking thing." He grinned. "We plan on making it very public. She's tired of it, too."

I nodded, feeling like that was a long way away. There were so many ways we could get caught now.

"I promise, Hannah. It's not going to be like this forever," he continued. "I don't like all the sneaking around either. I want to be able to take you out to dinner and kiss you on the street."

I liked the idea of that. I could see us walking hand in hand down main street. It was a pretty picture.

"You promise?" I asked, feeling like I was asking Santa Claus for a pony. It seemed like something that couldn't come true.

"Promise. We can come up with something about the boss/work thing. Dr. Taggert married his medical assistant, so I don't think he has much of a leg to stand on," Jacob told me. "As long as we do this properly and there's no damage to the image of the clinic, he won't care."

I sighed. I had that impossible feeling again.

"Come to the couch with me," he said, his voice going low and full of honey. I looked up to see a sexy grin on his face. "Maybe I can convince you there."

"Uh huh." I crossed my arms and gave him a fake frown. "Or maybe you're just trying to distract me."

His grin widened and his eyes glimmered with desire. "I guess you'll just need to come find out then."

"I guess I will." I grinned, made sure the door was locked and the shutters drawn, and went to the couch for him to convince me.

CHAPTER 18

The next three weeks flew by. I started keeping a quiet count of the days until Katie returned from filming. She kept progressing in her baking competition, so the date kept getting pushed further and further back.

I tried not to let it get to me, but it was hard. I wanted to be able to go out to dinner with Jacob without having to invite Donna every time. I wanted to start on us really being a couple. Right now, it things felt more like a really long, really awesome, one night stand. I didn't like living a lie, even if it wasn't really a lie.

"Any plans this evening, Donna?" Dr. Matthews asked as we tidied up the clinic and prepared to shut down for the evening.

"We have baseball tonight," Donna replied. "I'll be glad when the season is over. Going out to those fields in this heat is brutal. What about you, Hannah?"

"Just heading home. I have a really yummy recipe for a grilled chicken salad that I'm trying tonight. I got all the ingredients at the farmers market this morning." In code, that meant: *My place. Tonight. I'm making dinner.*

135

"That sounds delicious," Dr. Matthews commented. Code: *I'm coming.*

"I'll be sure to give you the recipe," I told him. Code: *Oh, you will be.*

"I'd appreciate that." The code on that was pretty self explanatory.

"How is Karina's daughter doing?" Donna asked.

"Great. You'd never even know she had surgery. She's all spunk and is so proud of her new scar," I said with a laugh. "She has decided she's going to be a surgeon when she grows up now so she can do this surgery all the time."

Both Donna and Jacob laughed.

We finished up our evening tasks and all headed out to the parking lot. I got in my car, Donna got in her truck, and Jacob got on his motorcycle. He looked so damn sexy it was hard not to drool. The man looked good in leather and on a bike.

We each went down the road until it split and we had to turn. Donna went left, I went right, Jacob went straight.

I drove home as he circled back around, taking a dirt road through a corn field and making sure that no one saw him. Finding secret routes to one another's houses was almost a game now. I knew three unlisted roads through corn fields that I could use to sneak over to his house. If I rode my bicycle, I didn't even have to leave the fields half the time. The bike also had the benefit of being easy to hide.

It was fun in a way, and depressing in another. As much fun as sneaking around was, it was hard. Some days I just wanted to be able to drive to his house, have a beer, and not worry about who saw my damn car there.

Once home, I started prepping things for our salad tonight. I had a bunch of different kinds of lettuce all straight from a local farm. There were fresh grown tomatoes, cucumbers, carrots, and even some local feta cheese. I made a balsamic dressing and turned the grill on for the chicken.

I was just putting the chicken on the grill when Jacob rolled up. He tucked his motorcycle under my weeping willow tree, using the dense leaves to hide it. While it wasn't visible from the road, it was visible from the house. I felt like we needed to find a better spot.

"Smells good," he said, taking off his helmet and coming out to the grill. "I'm starving."

"Good, because I made tons. Here, I have more veggies to chop," I replied. He took the fork and tongs from me to take over grilling.

I hummed as I went to the kitchen and finished getting everything ready. It felt so domestic and peaceful. I could imagine life always being like this.

Jacob came in and I cut up the chicken and we ate dinner at my kitchen. The conversation was good and we ended up laughing through the entire meal. He was so easy to talk to and he had the most amazing stories from his time in med school. I loved that he treated me like an equal. He appreciated me.

I put the dishes in the sink and he wiped down the table and took care of the grill. I appreciated it, because I hated scraping the grill and making sure the coals were out. I would much rather take care of dishes than deal with that.

It was just one more example of how we made the perfect team.

Thunder rumbled overhead.

"I'm going to grab my stuff off the bike," Jacob said, peering out the window at the sky. It didn't look too dark, but it was a good idea to grab his stuff just in case.

I followed him to the back door of the kitchen as he ran out and took a small side bag off his motorcycle. He stepped out from under the shelter of the tree and the sky suddenly let loose.

A torrential downpour came down, soaking him as he sprinted to the house. He clutched his bag to him, trying to keep it as dry as possible, but given how the rain was coming down, I wasn't sure how successful he was going to be.

"Are you okay?" I asked as he stumbled inside and I shut the door. His t-shirt was plastered to his chest like a second skin. I could see every line of his chest and abs.

"I'm fine," he replied, running his fingers through his hair. Little droplets of water scattered all over the floor. "Let me check my bag and make sure everything is still dry."

He set the bag on the kitchen floor and undid the zipper. Out came his white doctor coat and a stethoscope, as well as a change of scrubs and a set of medical journals.

"Good, the magazines are dry," he said, setting them carefully up on a table. "Dr. Taggert loaned them to me."

I shook my head and picked up the stethoscope. A very naughty idea entered my head. I got up, walked to my living room and made sure the door was locked. Then I came back to the kitchen where Jacob had put everything but the stethoscope neatly back in his bag.

"Hey, would you wear this for me?" I asked, holding the stethoscope up. Jacob frowned but took it and draped it over his shoulders.

"But you're all wet. You should take off your shirt," I said with a coy smile. It took him a second to understand what I was saying, but then he flashed me a sexy smile.

"Of course, Nurse Hannah," he said in a low voice that sent sexy shivers down my spine.

He pulled his wet shirt up and over his head. The shirt clung to the curves of his muscles as he tossed it to the floor. It landed with a splat. He left it there and adjusted his stethoscope.

I forgot how to breathe looking at him. His muscles glistened with rainwater. His pants hung around his hips, showing off his lean lines and trim waist. He kicked off his shoes.

"So, you want to play doctor?" he asked, holding onto his stethoscope and grinning seductively at me.

"Let's go up to the exam room," I replied breathlessly.

"Lead the way, Nurse Hannah."

I hurried up the stairs to my room, skipping along with excitement.

I sat down on my bed as Jacob followed me into my room.

"I'm going to need to do a full exam," he said, closing the door behind him. "Please remove your clothing."

"Of course, Doctor."

I stood up and slowly lifted my shirt up and over my head. I loved the way his eyes followed my movements. I could see the excitement growing in his pants as he watched me strip. I made each movement slow and deliberately as sexy as possible.

"Pants too," he murmured, his eyes watching my body. His gaze was anything but clinical.

I stood before him, completely naked. There was no self-consciousness to it, though. I felt sexy standing there with my hand on my hip and a coy smile on the face.

Jacob licked his lips. "I'm going to need to listen to your heart. Have a seat on the bed. Do you mind if I get more comfortable?"

I nodded and sat gingerly on the edge of the bed like I would at a real exam.

He slid out of his wet pants, kicking them to the side. They slid under my bed. His underwear were still mostly dry, but he took those off as well.

Good lord did that man look good naked.

He put the stethoscope in his ears. "Let me listen to your heart."

He put the cold bell of the stethoscope on my chest, groping one of my breasts in the process. I moaned slightly as he felt me up, still moving the stethoscope. I was sure he could hear my heart pounding with excitement and lust.

"Sounds excellent," he murmured, leaning forward and kissing my bare shoulder. I shuddered with want at his touch.

"I'm so glad. I knew I needed an expert medical opinion."

"I think we need to test your heart rate out a little more. Lay down for me."

I lay back on the bed, my head on the pillow.

Jacob took the stethoscope from his ears and draped it over his shoulders again. "Spread your legs, please."

I quickly did as he asked.

"Excellent. Now for the exam." He caressed my breasts before following the curves of my hips. He traced his fingers across my stomach down to my open legs.

The man knew his anatomy. He found my pleasure center in less than a second. I gasped as he sent a surge of sensation that ran up my spine and tingled out to my finger tips.

"You have excellent responses," he said, sliding a finger into me. His fingers knew exactly where to touch. My hips arched upward, and I moaned with delight. His skilled hands thrust and sought my depths.

Quicker than I thought possible, I was there. He pulled pleasure through my veins, filling me with overwhelming sensation. I started to tremble.

"Come for me," he whispered, his fingers bringing even more pleasure. "Let me see you."

With a gasp, I crested the mountain to orgasm. His hand kept working, thrusting and filling me with his fingers to cause me unbearable pleasure.

"I can see that your nervous system is working appropriately," he murmured as I lay shuddering on the bed before him.

"I think you need to do some further exams," I gasped. I looked down at his massive erection, just waiting to give me more pleasure.

He grinned and reached for the stash of condoms I now kept in my nightstand. It was on in a second, and he was up on the bed with me.

"The doctor is in," I whispered as he slid into me. I giggled, but it quickly turned into a moan.

"Holy shit," he said reverently as he filled me, his voice trailing off and the sounds blending together.

It gave me a rush to know I reduced this smart, sexy man to nothing more than single syllables. He lost himself to me, letting himself go as he could with no one else.

We moved slowly at first. I reached up and grabbed the stethoscope, using it to pull him further into me. It was leverage that I gladly utilized to have even more of him.

I kissed him, breathless and needful. I looked up to see that he was watching me with dark eyes. He needed me as much as I needed him. I let go of the stethoscope and wrapped my arms around his neck.

He held onto the headboard, using it as his own leverage to thrust deeper into me. My hips arched and bucked into him, wanting even more of him. He filled me completely, yet I wanted more. I couldn't get enough of him, even when he was hilt deep.

"More, Doctor," I whispered. He thrust harder.

"Anything you want, Nurse," he gasped.

He sat up and with a smooth motion flipped me onto my stomach. He pressed his hand into my low back and skewered me. I cried out as he filled me from a new direction.

He was in complete control with his hand on my lower

back. I could writhe, but he set the pace. I moaned into the pillow, losing myself to his every thrust.

"Hannah," he groaned. He swelled, his fingers digging into my hips as he put me in the spot that felt best for him.

With a guttural cry, he lost himself to me completely.

Best doctor's appointment ever.

CHAPTER 19

*I* lay on the bed and panted for breath.

That was quite possibly the hottest sex I'd ever had in my life.

"That was amazing, Dr. Matthews," I finally gasped. I rolled over to see him grinning at me.

"I didn't know that the doctor thing did it for you," he teased. "Now I know why you jumped my bones at the clinic."

I gave his shoulder a gentle push. "*You* jumped *my* bones," I told him.

He laughed and reached for me, apparently ready for another session of jumping.

That's when I heard the unmistakable sound of my front door opening, followed by my mother's voice.

"Hannah? Are you home?"

Jacob and I looked at one another and our eyes got big. My mother was a founding member of the Ladies' Bridge Club. If she saw us together, we'd be toast.

We both scrambled off the bed. I grabbed an old robe

143

hanging off my nightstand and wrapped it around me. Jacob jumped into his underwear and opened my window.

"It looks like it's just her. I don't see your dad in the car," he whispered. He frowned as he looked around the room at the mess we had made. "My clothes are all wet."

"He could still be here, so be careful," I hissed. "You have the scrubs in my kitchen. The kitchen door should still be open."

Apparently it didn't matter if I locked my doors.

"*Should* be open?" he asked, not looking thrilled at the prospect of getting stuck outside my house in only his underwear.

"Hannah? Are you upstairs?" My mother's voice echoed up the stairs. She was nearly to my door.

We didn't have time to come up with a better plan.

I motioned to Jacob to go out the window. At least it wasn't raining anymore. He slipped out onto the roof just as my mother threw open my bedroom door.

"There you are. Why was your door locked?" she asked me as if she hadn't just barged into my house, let alone my bedroom, unannounced.

"Because I don't want random people walking into my house," I said, crossing my arms. "You could have called."

"I did. You didn't pick up."

I checked my watch. It couldn't have been more than an hour that I didn't check my phone. Seriously, mother?

"What was so important that you came all the way over here?" I asked, doing my best to keep my thin robe wrapped discreetly around me. I could see the edges of Jacob's wet jeans poking out from underneath my bed. I just hoped my mother didn't look too closely.

"What were you doing? You're all flushed." She frowned and put the back of her hand on my forehead.

I was having hot, kinky sex, mother, I wanted to say. But I didn't. I didn't feel like dying today.

"Exercising." It was close to the truth. Jacob did give me a good workout and I would be sore in all the right places later.

"Oh. Well, whatever you're doing is working," mom said, looking me up and down. "You're practically glowing."

"Um. Thanks."

"But, why are you naked?" she asked again, pointedly looking at my thin little robe.

"Because I was just about to shower," I replied. "I just exercised, got all sweaty, wasn't looking at my phone, and was just about to get in the shower."

It sounded surprisingly reasonable considering I made it up on the fly.

"Well, I need you to come to the house with me," my mom said. She fiddled with the purse strap over her shoulder. For a moment, she lost her confidence. "It's your dad."

The pit of my stomach fell out.

"What happened?" I asked, fear starting to fill my middle.

"It's not a big deal, but he fell this afternoon. He says he's fine, but I don't believe him." She tugged harder on the purse strap.

Cold washed over me despite the open window and the hot humid air flowing in.

"I'm going to get dressed. Will you step into the hall and tell me more?" I asked my mom.

"Of course." She readjusted her purse and stepped out into the hallway, keeping the door between us cracked open. I ran around my room looking for clothes that were clean and belonged to me.

With my mom no longer in the room, I turned to the window to see Jacob by his bike pulling up his scrub pants. At least he was dressed now. He looked up and made a question motion. I quickly shook my head and pushed the window down.

"Your dad was working out in the garage. I hadn't heard from him and it was dinner time, so I went to get him. He was on the floor and couldn't get up. He was just so weak." She paused and took a deep breath. "He says he's just tired and to let him rest. He didn't want me to bother you, but... I'm worried and I just don't know what to do."

I swallowed down the cold dread and slipped a soft t-shirt over my head. I gave myself a second to take a deep breath before putting on a smile for my mother.

"I'll help," I promised, opening my bedroom door. "That's why I'm here."

"I know, and I'm so glad." My mom smiled sadly. She shook her head and sniffled, then put on a chipper smile to cover her fear. "Did I see Dr. Matthews bike under your tree? It's a good spot to keep it out of the rain."

"Uh...." *Shit. Shit. Shit. Shit. Come up with a reasonable explanation, Hannah....* "He's, uh, he's here helping me with something. Outside."

"He's such a gentleman," my mother replied. "Always helping everyone."

"Yeah. That's it." I forced a smile. "I'm going to go let him know I'm leaving." I was already halfway down the stairs. How did my mother see his bike? Was her x-ray vision from my childhood still intact?

I sprinted out the unlocked front door.

"Jacob, she knows you're here," I whispered as loud as I dared, running toward the tree. I found him under the tree with sex hair and despite the fact that my mother wasn't far behind me, all I could think about was jumping his bones again.

"How much did she see?" he asked, pinking slightly in his cheeks.

"Just your bike here," I replied. "I told her you were helping me."

He nodded.

"Oh, hello Mrs. O'Leary." Jacob smiled at the person behind me. It was his disarming, oh-so-charming smile that he used to use on teachers he wanted to get out of trouble with and girls he wanted to impress. "It's lovely to see you."

"Dr. Matthews, it's always a pleasure," my mom replied, blushing slightly. His smile could charm old ladies, that's for sure. And young ladies, too. "What are you helping Hannah with?"

"She thought there might be a raccoon in the tree out here." He was a smooth liar. That was far better than anything I had in mind for why he was out under a tree.

"Really?" She turned to me and gave me a gentle swat on the arm. "You didn't say anything. You know your dad is always happy to help with that kind of stuff."

"I, uh, I didn't want to bother him," I replied. That's when I noticed that Jacob didn't have shoes on. He was barefoot in the dirt. I sent a silent plea up to the universe that my mother wouldn't notice. "So, Jacob. I mean, Dr. Matthews. I mean, Jacob. I need to go help my mom. Are you good here on your own?"

"You know the way to get rid of raccoons is to play talk radio at them all day and night. They can't stand the stuff. To be honest, neither can I. I would move out of someone's chimney if an angry man was yelling politics at me all night, too," my mom said, not moving. She looked up at the tree and frowned. "I don't know if that would work outside, though."

"I actually don't think there are raccoons," Jacob replied. "Maybe just a squirrel. Or a bird."

We made eye contact and he shrugged. I stifled an inappropriate laugh. Apparently there were squirrels in my tree.

And birds. I felt so obvious that I was sure my mother would see right through both of us.

"A squirrel would be easier to deal with," my mother agreed.

"Mom, we should go." I tugged gently on her arm. I was afraid she would notice that Dr. Matthews wasn't wearing shoes. Or that he had sex hair and a twinkle in his eye that would give us both away. My mom always figured out my secrets. The last thing I wanted was for her to get close to this one.

"Right." My mom flashed Jacob another smile. "Thanks for helping out my Hannah. Have a good evening, Dr. Matthews."

"Bye, Dr. Matthews," I chimed in, guiding her toward her car.

"Bye, Mrs. O'Leary. Bye, Hannah." He leaned against his bike with a confident smirk that made me want to shake my head.

We had gotten so close to being discovered and somehow managed to escape notice. My stomach was twisting with fear of getting caught and the news that my dad needed me.

I made sure my mom got in her car and backed out before starting my engine. Jacob gave me one last wave as I left the man I was sleeping with to follow my mother back home.

# CHAPTER 20

"Hey, Dad," I said softly, coming up behind him.

He sat dozing in his easy chair in front of the TV. The news was on low, but he wasn't paying attention to the day's stock market prices. He snored slightly and then shook himself awake.

"Hannah." He smiled a little, then frowned. "What are you doing here?"

"I came to check on you," I told him, coming around and kneeling in front of his chair. I set my first aide kit on the floor next to me.

He looked pale, and when I put my hand on his, he felt clammy. Despite the air conditioning going in the house he was sweating, but had a blanket across his lap. I didn't like the slight wheeze in his voice when he spoke, either.

"I'm fine," he assured me. "I just need some rest."

"Mom told me you fell today," I replied.

"I just got light headed. It's all those damn medications and the damn humidity right now," he grumbled. "I just need some rest is all. I'm fine."

"Okay. You rest, and I'll check you out." I

He narrowed his eyes at me, and I thought he was going to protest. He opened his mouth and then just sighed. "Fine."

It was a bad sign. My father was too tired to argue with me. This was a man that loved to talk politics, religion, farming techniques, and guns. The fact that he put up no resistance made my internal alarms go off.

He opened his mouth to say something, but instead of words just coughed. It sounded wet and heavy. He struggled to take a deep breath and for a moment, I was worried he'd stop breathing entirely. No wonder he was exhausted if just breathing took that much energy.

I opened my kit and pulled out my things to do a full nursing assessment. I had a blood pressure cuff, a thermometer, stethoscope, bandages, ace wraps, and all sorts of various creams in my kit. It seemed that once people found out I was a nurse, they always wanted me to check their blood pressure or look at a cut to see if it was infected.

I did a full nursing assessment on my father and didn't like the results.

He had several abrasions on the palms of his hands from catching himself in the fall, as well as a small bump on his head. They were minor, so I wasn't too worried about them. His heart rate was too fast and he had a low grade fever, but the most concerning thing I found were his lung sounds.

Every breath crackled and wheezed. Add in his weakness and loss of energy, I was fairly confident he had pneumonia again.

I hated the way my chest tightened around my heart. We'd found his cancer because of pneumonia. It was the reason he'd gone to the clinic two years ago and they'd seen concerning shadows in his lungs. It was the first test in a long line of doctor appointments, specialist appointments, and chemo and radiation treatments.

And now he had it again.

Dad had dozed off while I listened to his lungs, and I let him stay there, sitting upright in his chair to go talk to my mother. Mom stood in the kitchen, watching me carefully. Her mouth was a thin line and her arms crossed.

"So?" she asked as I walked over.

"I think he's got pneumonia," I said softly.

She blinked back sudden tears, but none fell. I knew that this was perhaps the hardest on her. This man was her everything. They'd married at eighteen, had one daughter after years of trying, and had been through everything together.

"What do we do?" she asked me, her eyes going to the easy chair.

"I'm going to call Dr. Matthews and have him meet us at the clinic. We need to do a chest x-ray to make sure it is pneumonia. If it is, he'll write a prescription for antibiotics. We'll do a breathing treatment in the office, and that will make him feel a lot better."

My mother nodded, taking in a deep breath. She stoically lifted her chin up and squared her shoulders. My mother was a strong woman.

"Okay. I'll get the car." She uncrossed her arms and hurried to her purse. I saw her quickly wipe at her eyes as she went to the garage. I called Jacob and told him what I suspected. He promised to meet me at the clinic immediately.

I closed my eyes and took a breath in. This wasn't easy for me. This wasn't just another patient. This was my father. This was the man that danced with me at every cousin's wedding because I didn't have a date. This was the man that taught me how to change a tire and catch a fish. This man loved me and I adored him.

I went and gently touched his arm. "Dad? Time to wake up. Dr. Matthews needs to see you."

He snorted as he slowly woke. "I just want to sleep," he mumbled.

"I know, but you don't want to disappoint Dr. Matthews," I said, pulling on his arm.

He sighed, but got up. "My shoes are by the door."

I held his arm, surprised at the amount of weight he rested on me. He struggled with his steps, his body obviously exhausted. I helped him to the door and we slid on a pair of slippers rather than dealing with shoes. Mom waited outside for us, the car door open and ready for him.

Dad slept on the way to the clinic. Mom and I tried some light easy conversation for a few minutes, but neither one of us was really interested in actually talking. She put on the radio to an oldies station and we drove without saying anything.

Dr. Jacob was waiting outside the clinic when we arrived. He'd kept on the scrubs from earlier, but had smoothed his hair and wore shoes now. I felt better just seeing him.

"Good evening, Mr. O'Leary," Jacob greeted my father. He helped my father stand from the car. Jacob took most of his weight, supporting my father even when his legs gave out. My father was weaker than I had thought.

My mother and I followed behind the two men into the clinic. My mother kept a calm face, but she alternated between twisting her wedding ring around on her finger and tugging on her purse strap. She was far more nervous than she was letting on, too.

Inside, Dr. Matthews set my father up at the x-ray machine. My father struggled to keep upright as the machine buzzed. I could hear his labored breathing and my own lungs tried to compensate for him.

For the first time, I really felt that my father was sick. I knew he had cancer. I'd seen the x-rays. I'd gone to the chemo appointments with him. I'd talked to all his doctors, but had never felt this real before. He'd always been so strong, so big, and so indestructible. He was a rock in my life. In my mind, he was as invincible as Superman and twice as strong. I remembered him throwing me up above his head and catching me. In my mind, he was still capable of doing that despite the fact I was well over thirty years old.

To see him struggle to stand was at odds with the man I held in my mind. It was impossible that the two men where the same, and yet I knew they were.

I had to turn away and close my eyes. I didn't want to see this. Not yet. Not ever, really.

"Hannah, will you set up the breathing treatment?" Dr. Matthews asked, coming out into the hallway. His eyes were kind as he put his hand on my shoulder.

"Yeah. Sure. Sorry, I didn't even think about starting it," I said, trying to shake myself out of daughter mode and into nurse mode.

"Hey, are you okay?" Jacob asked, standing in front of me and putting his hands on my shoulders. My mother had disappeared into the x-ray room now that the pictures were taken, so we were alone in the hallway.

"I don't know," I answered honestly, looking up at him. "I know what's going to happen next. I know how to give the medications. I know the techniques. I know the care plan, but..."

"But, it's different when it's someone you love," he finished for me. I nodded and he wrapped his arms around me.

I placed my ear on his chest, closing my eyes. Jacob's steady heartbeat and the strength of his arms held me still, even as my world threatened to spin out control. In his embrace, I was safe.

"You going to be okay?" he asked me softly, his breath soft against my hair.

I nodded, still holding tightly onto him. I appreciated that he didn't let me go. He was waiting for me to let go first.

Slowly, I took a deep breath and relaxed my grip on him. My mother could walk out at any moment, and even though I knew we could spin it, I didn't want her to see us. I didn't feel like defending myself against the will of the Ladies' Bridge Club tonight.

"I'll go get the breathing treatment," I murmured. He gave my shoulders a gentle squeeze before turning to go check on the x-rays.

I went to an exam room and set up the tubing and medications. He would wear a mask and breath in medications that would open his lungs and let him breathe better. I knew how to set these up as we did them often, yet my fingers slipped and twisted on the tubes like I was a novice.

Finally, I brought my dad in and set him up. He struggled with the mask at first, but when I told him the medicine would help him breathe, he gave it a good attempt. Within a few breaths, I could see the tension relax slightly from his shoulders as the medicine started to work on his body.

I left my mother watching my father, and stepped out into the hallway. Dr. Matthews came around the corner. He gave me a gentle, soft smile, and then, since no one was around, a hug.

"It's pneumonia," he told me, his voice low. I nodded into his shoulder. I'd known it the moment I heard his lungs.

"Thank you for being here," I whispered. I was clutching at him again.

"Of course," he replied. "I'm always here for you, and not just because it's my job."

I looked up into his pale eyes and he kissed my forehead. I felt loved. He was my protector. He rode a motorcycle, kicked ass in the clinic, and he loved me.

He gave me one more squeeze before going to the exam

room to talk with my parents. I heard his low voice as he told them the results of the x-ray. He answered questions about the antibiotics and medications he was sending home with them.

I peeked through the open door to see my mother sitting next to my father, her hands wrapped around his. He looked smaller now than I remembered. Frailer. My mother sat with her back perfectly straight as she nodded to Dr. Matthews' words.

I leaned against the hallway and closed my eyes.

The whole reason I was in Iowa was to take care of my father. I had known what was coming from the moment I'd agreed to come.

Yet, it was different now that it was happening. It was so much harder. I didn't have my clinical detachment to keep me sane. This was going to be so much harder than I expected.

But, at least I had Jacob. I could hear his voice, soothing and calm, as he spoke to my parents. Just hearing him made my heart ache just a little bit less. I knew that he would help me when my clinical facade cracked and I needed to be a daughter rather than a nurse to my father.

I knew that he would be there for me. I knew it deep in the core of my bones, and it gave me comfort knowing that I wasn't alone anymore.

I had someone now.

# CHAPTER 21

"So, we're breaking up today," Jacob announced.

I looked across the bed at him and raised an eyebrow. Both of us were still completely naked and tangled up in his sheets. We'd been laying there all morning, simply enjoying laying in bed and playing on our phones together. Breaking up seemed like an odd thing to do at this point.

"Um, we are?"

"Not you," he explained, holding up his phone. "Katie and I. We're doing it today."

A small thrill went through me. This was the first step to Jacob and I being able to actually date. We would need to let the town settle down for a little bit after this, but hopefully I would stop getting mean looks from all the old ladies any time I even mentioned his name in public.

"How's it going to happen?" I asked him, leaning back in his very comfortable bed.

"At the bakery. Lunchtime."

"It'll be crowded. Nice." I nodded my approval.

"Want to come?" He grinned at me. "Katie says she's been

practicing crying and she made special cupcakes to throw at my head."

"Now I'm definitely not gonna miss it," I told him. "I hope she doesn't miss."

"Promise to help me mend my broken heart?" He gave me a sly smile.

I laughed. "I'll certainly help you with something," I replied, tugging at the sheets.

"You must be starving," Donna observed later in the day. "You've checked your watch three times since I said it was almost lunch."

"Jacob is buying us lunch from Katie's Bakery," I replied, trying to sound nonchalant. "I've been saving up my calories all day for this."

Donna narrowed her eyes. "You and the doc seem to be getting friendly."

"Donna, we went to school together. And yes, we are friends. We are also co-workers." I smiled at her. "And besides, he's with Katie, right?"

"Right." She nodded. "He would always do right by Katie. He's a good man."

I tried not to do a little happy dance. He was about to do right by Katie.

Finally, the last patient left and we were able to take our break. Donna flipped the sign to closed as Jacob gave me a wink and a nod. I practically skipped the entire way to Katie's Bakery.

Jacob refused to tell me what exactly was going to happen. He said that he wanted to have an honest reaction from me. All I knew was what he told me: she was planning on throwing cupcakes.

I made sure to wear something easily washed. I noticed that Jacob was wearing his least favorite pair of scrubs.

Katie's Bakery was packed. It was the middle of the lunch rush and it seemed like everyone in town was there.

I couldn't wipe the stupid grin off my face.

We stood in line with Donna asking why we couldn't skip to the front. Jacob was dating the owner, after all. Jacob just said that it wasn't right.

We ordered our food, and that's when the show began.

Katie came out and pulled Jacob out of line. She looked actually pissed. They started out with whispers in the corner that slowly escalated into yells.

"I never said that," Jacob growled.

"You're just jealous of my success," Katie yelled at him. "You can stand to be the one not in the spotlight."

"I think you're confusing yourself with me. We call that 'delusional' in the medical world," Jacob shouted at her.

By this time, the entire restaurant had fallen quiet. Everyone had their heads pointed toward their food, but all eyes were on Katie and Jacob. I was having a hard time not smiling.

"How dare you," Katie hissed. "You aren't who I thought you were at all."

"That's because you're never here," Jacob replied, his voice full of venom. "You've changed."

"I've gotten better."

"That's not what I'd call it," Jacob sneered. "Delusional was a good word."

That's when she chucked a cupcake at his head. The whole room gasped as it exploded with cherry filling all over his face.

"That's it!" he screamed at her. "I'm done!"

"Good. I never want to see you're face in here again. You understand? We're through! I hate you! I hate your stupid face!" Her face twisted with rage and she chucked another cupcake at him, only this time he ducked and it exploded on the wall behind him.

"Screw you," he told her and stomped out of the bakery.

"Screw yourself!" she screamed at his back.

I looked around at all the patrons. Every mouth hung open in disbelief.

"Did they just break up?" Donna asked me, clutching her sandwich like a lifeline.

"I think so. It looked pretty brutal. Relationships don't come back from that kind of thing," I told her. "He's pretty anal about his hair and she really got him with that cupcake."

Donna just nodded, her mouth hanging open. I glanced around, making sure that several other of the Ladies' Bridge Club were present. Maybe this would convince them that Katie and Jacob weren't "practically engaged" anymore.

Katie quietly composed herself in the corner. "Sorry about that everyone."

She then fled to the back room.

"I'm going to go check on Jacob," I said to Donna, but she was still staring at the cherry filling on the wall in shock. A chunk of vanilla cupcake hit the floor with a splat.

I cut through the alley behind the Bakery and saw Katie leaning against a dumpster. It sounded like she was crying. I hurried over to check on her.

"Katie, are you okay?" I asked, touching her on the shoulder.

She turned and her eyes lit up with recognition. That's when I realized she wasn't crying. She was laughing. She was laughing so hard she could barely breathe.

She gave me a giant hug. "Jacob told me about you two. You're great for each other. I'm glad I could help." She let me go and wiped the tears on her face, leaving big flour smudges on both her cheeks. "That was incredibly cathartic."

"It was incredibly believable," I told her. "I don't think anyone has moved inside."

"Oh, I hope so. I had some of my LA friends coach me on what to do. You think the cherry filling was too much?" Her shoulders started shaking again as she thought of it.

"It was perfect," I told her. I gave her one more hug. "Thanks for breaking up with him."

"It was my pleasure," she replied with a laugh as more tears streamed down her cheeks. I let her be as she laughed behind her restaurant and I hurried back to the clinic.

Jacob was waiting for me in the break room.

"Good?" he asked, his smile beaming off his face. "Was I believable?"

"You were perfect," I told him. "I nearly believed you."

"Good." He grinned and kissed my cheek. "It's one step closer. It'll take some time, but Katie and I have agreed to be militantly hostile to one another for the next week. I really think this is going to work."

"Dr. Matthews? Dr. Matthews are you in here?" Donna called, making her way to the break room.

Jacob and I took a step away from one another just before Donna came in. Her face was full of worry.

"Dr. Matthews, are you okay?" she asked him.

"I'm pissed," he told her, sounding actually angry. "If you see her, you tell her it's off. I wouldn't be caught dead dating her. Do you see what she did to me?"

He pointed to the cherry filling coating his hair.

"Are you sure?" Donna asked him. "You two seemed so perfect..."

"Perfectly miserable," Jacob finished for her. "And yes. She's willing to humiliate me in public. I can't be with a woman like that."

"I'm so, so sorry Jacob." Donna patted his arm. "If you need anything..."

"I don't want to deal with her," Jacob growled. "She's no longer a patient here."

Donna's eyes went big. "But, that would mean she'd have to go to a different doctor."

"That's the point," Jacob told her. "She's not welcome here. I don't care if she's bleeding. You call her an ambulance and let them deal with it."

With that he turned and stomped into the bathroom, slamming the door shut as hard as possible.

"Wow. I think he's actually serious," Donna whispered. "That's so sad."

"Yeah. Definitely sad," I agreed, doing my best not to smile. If Donna believed it, then the rest of the Ladies' Bridge Club wouldn't be far behind.

We were one step closer to being together.

# CHAPTER 22

*I* smiled as I picked out groceries. I was heading over to Jacob's house this evening and he'd asked me to pick up a couple of things to help with dinner. I felt incredibly domestic and helpful as I picked the ripest tomatoes and the freshest gallon of milk in the entire store.

The summer heat was oppressive as I walked to my car. The blacktop radiated the sun and shimmered with imaginary mirages of water. I was sweating by the time I finished the short walk and loaded everything into my car.

That was summer in Iowa. Humid and hot.

The cicadas thrummed in the trees and birds called out as got in my car. We would get thunderstorms this evening, and given Jacob's propensity for getting wet and looking sexy as hell because of it, I was rather looking forward to them.

I especially liked how he held me as the thunder crashed around us. When the storms came, I didn't have to worry about people coming to our houses and finding us. I didn't have to worry about what anyone else thought. I was Jacob's and he was mine.

It was my own little slice of heaven.

I hummed as I drove the roundabout route to Jacob's house. I didn't want his father surprising me again. I had some dummy files in my car, just in case. I also had my notifications turned all the way up on my phone in case Jacob needed to text me that his parents had randomly showed up at his house.

We had a system and so far it had worked.

I circled a cornfield and double checked to make sure there was no one around before turning down the dirt road to Jacob's home. I tucked my car into his open garage and shut the door, feeling rather like a spy as I did it.

No one knew I was here.

"Groceries," I called out, entering the kitchen. Jacob emerged from the living room and smiled at me before taking them off my hands.

"These look great," he said, putting the tomatoes in a colander to wash and dry. "And so do you."

"Is that so?" I grinned. I always felt beautiful around Jacob. I didn't need to wear makeup or do anything crazy with my hair. I liked to, but I didn't have to. He thought I was beautiful no matter what the humidity was doing to my hair.

He wrapped his arms around my waist, resting his hands on my ass. A gentle squeeze told me exactly where his mind was.

In the gutter.

"So, that's first today, huh?" I asked, looking up through my eyelashes at him.

I loved the way he looked back at me. He looked at me like he was hungry and I was a five-course meal. His pupils dilated and he pulled me into a sensual kiss. I could feel him hardening against my hip and desire flared to life. The tomatoes could wait if he was what I could have instead.

"Yeah, I think that's first today," he whispered, nibbling on my ear. His breath tickled the small hairs of my neck and made me drunk on lust. I was jelly to his touch when he did that. "You drive me wild."

He tugged on my shorts, pulling them to the floor. I kicked them to the side as he ran his fingers along the smooth satin of my panties. I loved the way his skillful fingers danced across me, teasing me with the pleasure he could bring. I let my head fall back and groaned as he kissed my neck and played with the thin satin.

"More, please," I whimpered, lifting the back of his shirt. He grinned and pulled it up and over his head. I don't know if they taught men the sexiest way to remove their shirts in a secret boy school or if it just came naturally, but I loved watching him strip for me.

I ran my fingers up and down his chest, feeling his heart beat underneath my palm. He pressed his hips into mine and I could feel just how hard he had gotten in just a few minutes. I ached to feel him inside of me. I needed it.

My hands slid down his chest to his waist and undid the button on his khaki shorts. I helped guide the shorts off his hips and down to the ground. I went to my knees and looked up at him with a smile. I saw his breath catch just a little as I licked my lips.

I reached up to grab the hem of his boxers when I saw his mother watching us with horrified eyes.

I froze. I didn't know what to do. Maybe she was actually a T-Rex and couldn't see me if I didn't move.

We both stood perfectly motionless for an unbearable amount of time.

"What's wrong, baby?" Jacob asked, looking down with a frown. He followed my look of terror to see his mother standing in his kitchen with a bag of cucumbers. "Oh shit."

That's when his mother came alive.

"Oh shit?" she repeated.

"Mom, what are you doing here?" Jacob managed to keep

a relaxed body posture despite the fact that he was standing in his boxers, his erection quickly fading. I still was on my knees in nothing but my panties and t-shirt. I didn't think I could get up.

Mrs. Matthews focused the full weight of her glare on me. I swear her eyes went red and smoke came out of her ears. She was shorter than me, but at that moment she towered over me.

"Get out," she growled, marching over and grabbing the collar of my shirt. She was tiny, but strong as she managed to nearly drag me out of Jacob's kitchen.

"Mom, what are you doing?" Jacob moved in front of her and blocked her path. "You don't talk to her like that."

"I'll talk to that *whore* any way I like," she spat. She let go of my collar, pushing me away in the process before looking up at her son. "How could you do this, Jacob?"

"Do what, Mom?" Jacob crossed his arms, the muscles standing out as he protected me from his mother.

"Do this to Katie." Mrs. Matthews shook her head in horror. "You're supposed to be getting engaged soon. What will poor Katie think?"

"Katie and I aren't a couple," Jacob told her. "We broke up."

"Because of her?" She made a face that made me feel like garbage.

"No. Because Katie and I aren't right for each other. It's over. I can see anyone I want to see and I want to see Hannah."

Mrs. Matthews sighed. "You say that, but I see the way you and Katie are around each other. That's a partnership worth pursuing." Her gaze came back to me and she twisted her mouth like she'd bitten into something bitter. "You sure jumped on the availability. He's barely been single for an hour. Learn that in the city?"

"You don't talk that way to Hannah," Jacob growled.

"Jacob, you clearly aren't thinking clearly." His mother smiled at him and patted his shoulder. "This is a fling. This doesn't mean anything."

"You're wrong." His voice was solid and sure. It made my heart thrill to hear him defend me. "You need to get out of my house. Now. You don't talk to Hannah like that."

"Jacob-"

"Get out of my house." His tone was dangerous.

She crossed her arms and her mouth tightened as she looked back and forth between Jacob and me.

"Fine." She huffed to the door. "This isn't over. I won't let you throw everything I worked so hard on away for a blow-job."

Jacob's mother slammed the door hard enough that the entire house shook. Silence filled the room. I could hear her car engine start and she pulled away, the gravel crunching in her tires.

Jacob was at my side, his hands on my shoulders and his blue eyes searching my face.

"Are you okay? I can't believe she said any of that," he told me. He looked confident, but his hands were shaking. "None of that was okay."

"It's not your fault," I told him, rising slowly to my feet. "I appreciate you defending me."

"I wanted to punch her," he admitted.

"Not a good thing to do to your mother," I informed him. I was glad he managed to crack a small smile.

"I'm sure this will blow over," he said, but it was obvious he didn't believe it.

"You know that's not going to happen, right?" I pulled my shorts back up. I didn't feel like a sex goddess anymore. "She's going straight to the Ladies with this. It's going to be all over town by morning."

My voice caught as I thought of what was going to happen.

"I'm so sorry, Jacob."

"For what?" He wrapped his arms around me. "I'm as much in this as you are."

I shook my head. "You're the prodigal son returned. They are going to say that I lured you. That I tempted you down the wrong path. Two hundred years ago they'd have me hung as a witch."

"Hannah..."

I wiped at my face. "I should go home. I'm not going to be good company tonight."

"Please don't go." He looked at me with puppy-dog eyes. "I don't want you to leave. Stay. It's not like it can get worse, right?"

I sighed. He was right. His mother had just caught me about to give him a blow-job. Thank heaven it was then and not ten seconds later. Just thinking about it made my skin crawl and my stomach sick.

"I think I'm going to throw up." Nausea suddenly hit me hard and fast. I ran for the bathroom and barely made it.

I splashed some cool water on my face, but the queasiness remained. It had to be the stress and the worry. It had finally caught up with me. I was already imagining myself being kicked out of the grocery store, a scarlet letter emblazoned on my chest.

"Here." Jacob brought me a cool glass of water and a couple of Tums. I chewed on them gratefully and took a sip of water. "Come sit down."

I let him guide me to the couch and there he wrapped his arm around me. We watched TV and I tried not to look at my phone. I didn't want to know what was going to happen next.

I snuggled into his arms, and surprisingly started to drift off to sleep. I'd been tired recently.

"I love you," I whispered, not even realizing the words came out of my mouth. I froze, suddenly very awake.

He moved, pushing me up and putting his hands on either side of my face. I was sure he could feel the blush heating his palms. I bit my lip. I didn't mean to say it out loud, but it was still true. I loved him. I'd loved him since that science class in high school.

He smiled, his eyes soft and sparkling. He leaned forward and kissed my forehead.

"I love you," he whispered back and my heart stopped beating.

Jacob Matthews loved me. *Me.*

"Really?" I asked, my heart still frozen.

He nodded. "Yes." He kissed me again, this time on the mouth. It was soft and tender. "Always."

I fell into him, burying myself into his shoulder as he held me tight.

This was no longer the worst day of my life. Jacob loved me. It was now one of the best.

# CHAPTER 23

My stomach still hadn't settled from the night before. I hoped it wasn't food poisoning.

Jacob's phone went off and he groaned. We'd both fallen asleep on the couch watching TV and now the soft morning light filtered in. The "Are you still watching screen?" sat waiting for us to pick the next episode.

Jacob groaned and reached for his phone. It took him two tries to swipe it.

"I have to go into the office," he said, reading the message. "Jackie Rhodes needs stitches."

"Do you need help?" I asked. I didn't really want to go in to the office. I wanted to just hide in Jacob's house or possibly my bathtub and just never come out. I wouldn't have to deal with the consequences of us being found out that way.

"No. He's just busted his hand open on a piece of equipment again. It's the third time this year. He's got to get a guard or some gloves or something." Jacob stretched his arms up over his head and made the early morning stretch noise. "Want me to pick up some breakfast on my way back?"

I shook my head. The idea of breakfast didn't appeal to me.

"I actually need to get some groceries and things," I told him. "And there's some stuff I need to do around my house. Want to come by later?"

He smiled and kissed my forehead as he stood up. "Always."

I watched as he walked up the stairs and listened as he clomped around. I was trying to muster up the energy and the courage to leave the couch.

He came back down wearing scrubs. "I'll see you later, okay?"

He kissed me once more before heading out the door to go stitch up Jackie.

I sat listening to the clock in the hall tick away the minutes. Finally, I got up, grabbed my things and headed to the garage.

My car started and I drove into town. It was a Sunday morning, and much of the town was either at church or getting ready for church. My mother was probably there, learning of my sins from the other church ladies.

I swung my car by the grocery store and saw Abigail St. James in the parking lot. She saw me and her eyes narrowed. I saw the word, "slut" cross her lips before she dug in her bag for something to throw at me.

News travels fast in a small town and gossip travels even faster. I didn't stop at the grocery store. I didn't want Abigail to key my car while I picked up eggs.

Instead, I drove the thirty minutes to the next town where hopefully no one knew I was sleeping with the town doctor. Still, to be safe, I parked in the back where no one would notice my car. Unfortunately, that meant I would have to run farther if they came after me with pitchforks. I wasn't sure which was worse, but decided that pitchforks were slightly less likely.

No one said anything as I walked into the store and grabbed a cart. I was safe for now.

I wandered the aisles, ignoring the messages piling up from my mother, and buying anything I thought I would need for the next three weeks. There was a good chance I wouldn't be able to buy anything in town for the next few days and I didn't want to be unprepared.

I bought eggs and milk. I bought bread and tortillas. I bought toothpaste and shampoo. And while I was in the bathroom section, I realized that I probably needed tampons.

Except, I should have needed them last week.

I stopped dead in the middle of the aisle and did the mental math sixteen times. I was late. I was usually a perfect twenty-eight day cycle with no irregularities. But, this month I was five days late.

Slowly, my brain put the pieces together.

I had sex with Jacob without a condom and now I was five days late.

It wasn't just stress. I wasn't just late.

I was pregnant.

I wasn't sure if I should to laugh or cry. This was the worst timing in the entire world. I had dreamed of being pregnant, especially by Jacob, but in my mind there was always a ring involved.

Instead, I was pregnant to a man that the whole town wanted to marry someone else. I was already the harlot that stole him away, and this would only make things worse. I was trapping him now. I could only imagine the conniption fit Mrs. Matthews would have if she found out.

"Maybe you're just late," I whispered to myself. "Maybe it's just stress."

Except I knew it wasn't. I had morning sickness. My

breasts were tender. I was peeing like crazy. And I was tired.

I went down an aisle and picked up a pregnancy test. I was just glad I wasn't in Riversville. The last thing my poor reputation needed was to be seen buying a pregnancy test.

I didn't buy anything else and just hurried to check out. I did the self-checkout so that the cashier wouldn't see the test. It was probably paranoia, but I didn't want anyone in town to know that I even had an inkling that I was pregnant.

I hauled everything out to the far end of the parking lot and put my groceries away. The test stayed in my purse.

I did the speed limit home, not wanting to draw any attention to myself. I took the back roads. I took some of my sneaky paths so no one would see me.

I managed to get home without anyone really seeing me. I put everything away and then slowly climbed the stairs and sat in the bathroom staring at the box.

What if I was pregnant?

What would I do? What would Jacob do? I wasn't sure how he was going to react. It was one thing to say you wanted kids, but a totally different thing to find out you had one.

But we were going to be parents.

Part of me was terrified. This wasn't what I had planned. This was a complete surprise.

But another part of me was excited. Happy, even. I was pregnant.

I was going to be a mother. It was all I'd wanted for a very long time and now I had it. Granted, it wasn't the way I wanted it, but I wasn't about to turn it down.

I just had to make sure.

So I peed on a stick and paced the bathroom floor for two minutes until two pink lines showed up.

I was pregnant.

And suddenly, things just got way more complicated.

# CHAPTER 24

*I* stress baked the rest of the evening. Muffins, cookies, brownies, and I even attempted a double layer chocolate cake. It came out better than I expected and that made me feel a little bit better. I would have kept baking, but I ran out of flour and didn't have the guts to go into town and get more.

Jacob got pulled to the hospital for a patient after stitching up Jackie and he wasn't able to get back. Jacob had privileges at the local hospitals so that he could treat the patients he knew in the hospital setting along with the doctors there. The privileges also allowed him to deliver the town's babies at the hospital as well.

That night, his patient unfortunately took a turn for the worst, and Jacob didn't want to leave the hospital at all. I told him it was fine and that I would see him at the office in the morning.

I held the phone in my hand a long time after he hung up.

I had no idea how I was going to tell him I was pregnant, but I knew on the phone while one of his patients was dying was not the right time.

It was late and I was out of flour. I took a bath and then laid in bed trying to sleep. Unfortunately, despite feeling exhausted, my mind was too busy to rest.

My phone buzzed with messages from my mother. They were mostly things like: *call me. What have you done? I raised you better than this.*

I didn't answer any of them. I did get one text from my father.

> *You doing okay, kiddo?*

I felt pretty safe answering him.

> *I'm fine.*

> *Okay. I love you.*

His response made my heart hurt just a little bit less. At least there was one person in town that wasn't angry at me. My dad still loved me.

It made me remember when I was in high school. I was sure that I looked ridiculous. I was chunky and my hair was awful. Throw in some bad skin, braces, and being too smart for my own good, I wasn't very popular. But, every morning, my dad told me I looked pretty. He'd always pick something, like the clips in my hair or my shirt, and give me one good compliment to take through the day.

Some days, it was the only nice thing anyone said to me all day.

Today's compliment was that he loved me. It made me feel as good as it did then.

I dressed the next morning and made sure to take the time to do my hair and makeup nicely. If I was going to be crucified by the town, I could at least look nice while they did it. It gave me a sort or armor to know that if nothing else, I looked good.

The parking lot was empty of cars other than Donna's truck. I had brought the muffins with me as a peace offer. Donna liked muffins and these were some of my best. I wasn't expecting her to forgive me, but I hoped it would at least make the day a little bit smoother.

I took a deep breath and went inside.

Donna sat at her desk with a scowl. She looked up as I entered and her eyes glowed red. I swallowed hard. I'd never seen her this angry.

"I brought muffins," I said with a smile, setting them up on the desk. "Chocolate chip."

Donna slowly reached for the muffins and then dumped them in the trash next to her. She then resumed typing something on the computer.

I blinked back tears.

"Okay. I'll be in my office," I said quietly. She didn't even acknowledge that I'd said anything. She just kept typing away.

I left the door to my office open as I started up the computer and went about making sure the exam rooms were stocked and ready for the day. It helped to be moving. I hoped that we would have one of our usual busy Mondays. If we were busy, I wouldn't have time to sit and reflect on the mess I was currently in.

I was walking by the desk when Dr. Matthews walked in and greeted Donna. She didn't bother to even look up and acknowledge his presence. He frowned slightly.

"Donna, are you okay?" he asked, coming up to the desk.

He had dark circles under his eyes and wore pale green surgical scrubs with the hospital logo on the chest pocket. It looked like he had spent the entire night at the hospital before coming straight to the clinic. He carried an extra large thermos of coffee.

"Fine." She replied, still looking at her computer.

"Okay, then," Dr. Matthews shrugged. "This is gonna be a fun day."

He came around the desk and smiled at me, his face loosing some of the exhaustion.

"Good morning," I greeted him. I wanted to give him a kiss, but that would be inappropriate. I could see Donna watching us for any impropriety from the corner of her eye. "How was your night?"

"Hellish," he said, taking a swig of coffee. "But, he's stable. They found the bleed and he's in the ICU, but he's going to be okay."

"Oh, that's good." I felt a little relief. It would have been a really bad day otherwise.

"Yeah," he agreed. "I got a few hours of sleep in the on-call room. And a spiffy new pair of scrubs."

He pointed to his new clothing.

"Looks very nice," I told him. Donna made a coughing noise.

"I'm going to go check my email," Jacob said, rolling his eyes at Donna. He gave me another smile before taking his coffee to his office.

I finished my chores and checked my watch. It was well after nine in the morning, and I hadn't heard the door to the clinic chime other than Dr. Matthews coming in. I went out to find an empty waiting room. I checked my watch again just to make sure it wasn't broken. Usually, by nine we had three or four patients.

I stood there, staring out at the empty room and frowning.

"Donna, where are the patients?" I asked after a moment.

She turned in her chair. "Everyone canceled."

I blinked twice. "What?"

"No one wants to be treated by you or him," she replied coldly. "I'm only here for the paycheck."

I looked out again at the empty room and my heart sank. This was not good for Jacob's contract with Dr. Taggert. This was not good for either of us.

The phone rang and Donna picked it up.

"Riversville Doctor Office," she said, her voice warm and kind. It was a stark contrast to the cold tone she used with me. "Yes. Dr. Matthews is the only doctor in. Dr. Taggert will be in tomorrow. I'll make sure to book you with him." She paused. "Yes, I'll make sure Hannah isn't the one to get you. I'll bring you to your room myself. Thanks for the appointment."

I swallowed the growing lump in my throat. This wasn't fair. We didn't do anything wrong.

I fled to my office, hating the swirling emotions in the pit of my stomach. How was I going to fix this? I didn't know what to do. Granted, sleeping with my boss was not the best idea, but it didn't deserve this level of outrage from the community.

There was a soft knock on my open door and I turned to see Jacob leaning in my doorway. I loved the way he did that.

It was nonchalant and cool. He was so much cooler than I was.

"I hear we have no patients today," he said.

I nodded. "I'm sorry."

"Hey, you didn't tell the patients not to come."

"I need to talk to you about something. Something important." My hand hovered over my stomach, my thoughts on the tiny life growing in my belly. I needed to tell him sooner rather than later. If he lost the clinic, I would also lose my job. This child needed parents with jobs and a means to support it.

"Sure." Jacob frowned. "Go for it."

I could see Donna leaning back in her chair, eavesdropping on our conversation.

"Not here," I said softly. I motioned my head toward the desk.

He looked over and sighed. Donna's chair clunked down. "Can it wait until tonight?"

I nodded. I honestly still had months before anyone would even be able to tell. A few hours wouldn't hurt anything. I couldn't get more pregnant in the next eight hours.

He gave me a soft smile before pushing off the door frame and heading back to this office. I sighed and stared at my computer screen again.

It was going to be a long day.

# CHAPTER 25

We had exactly three patients all day. One was an out-of-towner that sprained her ankle, one of the local farmers that didn't care who saw him as long as he got his hand fixed up, and Emily Markins and her baby.

Little baby Dominic was growing in leaps and bounds. He knew how to smile and I loved him immediately. Emily told us that there wasn't anyone else she wanted him to be seen by. She didn't care about the drama.

"There are a lot of people in town that don't care," she told us after the exam. "The patients will come back. We all know and trust you both. I can't believe people are being this shallow."

It made me feel a little bit better. I knew we were still the best healthcare providers for fifty miles, but I also knew that this was going to take some time to blow over. I just wished the blowing would go a little bit faster.

Donna left without saying goodbye. We just heard the door chime and then her car drive off. Dr. Matthews and I finished up the last few things and then he locked up. I stepped outside to find my car had been egged.

It stunk. The heat and humidity had baked the eggs into my car. I stared at it for a moment. I'd never had anyone egg my car before. I wanted to cry, but I didn't want whoever did it to see that they got to me.

"Come on over to my place and we'll get that cleaned up," Jacob said. He wrapped his arm around me and gave me a gentle hug.

"Do you have food?" I asked, hiking my purse up on my shoulder.

He sighed and shook his head. "Nope. Do you?"

"Just cereal and brownies. I didn't do a great job shopping." Mostly because I got distracted by needing to buy a pregnancy test.

"We can grab some pizza on our way to my house. I'll drive us both," Jacob replied. He sounded confident. I was nervous. If Donna, who I considered my friend, was willing to trash my muffins, and someone had egged my car, I wasn't sure that going anywhere in public was a good idea.

"Is that a good idea?" I asked him.

He thought for a moment and then frowned at my car. Before saying anything he went to the back tire.

"It's our only idea," he informed me. "Someone deflated your tires."

I hurried around to see that my two rear tires were indeed very flat. Not only was my car covered in egg, it wasn't going anywhere. I only had one spare.

"It looks like they just deflated it. The tire doesn't look slashed," Jacob said, peering around at the black wheels.

"Wow. I'm so glad they had some decency," I said sarcastically.

Jacob got up and brushed his pants. "Pizza and home. You look tired."

I nodded. I felt tired.

Luckily, Jacob had brought his truck today. It was better

for the long drive to the hospital than the motorcycle. I climbed into the passenger seat and Jacob started the truck. Hot air rushed out as the air conditioning struggled to make up for the heat of the day.

We drove in comfortable silence to the pizza place. It had gone by a million different names throughout the years, but it always remained a pizza place.

Jacob's truck rumbled down the street. It felt like everyone turned and gave us the evil eye as we drove. I shrunk down into the passenger seat and tried not to notice. For the first time since moving here, I missed the anonymity of the big city.

Jacob pulled to a stop in front of the pizza restaurant.

"I'll go in and just get a quick to-go pizza," he said. "I'll be right back."

He flashed me a confident smile and headed inside. It felt like forever before he came out empty- handed.

"Pizza's not on the menu," he said, getting into the driver's seat. "I forgot that Loretta owns this place and is a founding member of the Ladies' Bridge Club."

"I have cake. And salad. That's healthy, right?" I didn't want to try another restaurant. I just wanted to go home and pretend that this wasn't happening.

I didn't want to believe that my home could be this cruel over something like this. Jacob and I were in love. We deserved some sighs about improper work behavior, maybe a stern lecture, but not this.

That's when Abigail knocked on Jacob's window.

"You two bring a bad name to our town," she yelled through the glass. "I want you to know I won't be coming to your office. I don't want you rubbing off on my kids."

She made a rude motion and continued in to the pizza place.

"Well, that's the pot calling the kettle black. Especially

since she had her first kid two months after getting married and had to run a DNA test to make sure it was Aiden's," Jacob said, watching her go inside.

"Really?"

"Yeah. It's in her record. Don't tell anyone. If they only knew the secrets I keep for this town." He shook his head. "You said something about cake?"

I smiled, feeling a pleasant warmth in my chest. Jacob knew every dirty misdeed in this town. He was the one they all came to when they needed something fixed. Yet, he never said a word about any of it. He had kept my dad's secret. He now trusted me with secrets. He was a good man.

He was my man.

"Yeah, let's go home."

There was something I needed to tell him.

# CHAPTER 26

My house was luckily quiet and untouched. I was half afraid that I'd find my yard full of toilet paper or my grass drawn on in spray paint.

We went inside and I smiled at how normal it felt to have Jacob come in behind me. I liked coming home with Jacob. I liked the way he held the door for me and I loved that I wasn't worried about who saw us. As much as it sucked having the town hate us, there were some perks.

I pulled out two plates and the chocolate cake I'd baked the night before. The frosting was lopsided and I had put the layers on funny, but it should taste good. Chocolate cake after a bad day is always a good thing.

I sliced two big pieces and set them on plates. It was a healthy dinner for sure.

Jacob took a big bite and groaned. "Good cake," he mumbled, some crumbs spilling onto his scrub top.

"Thanks." I didn't take a bite yet. "There's something I wanted to talk to you about."

He swallowed and stuffed another bite into his mouth. "You said that. What did you want to talk about?"

My hands started to shake and I thought I might throw up. I swallowed hard. I knew people usually came up with a cute way to tell their significant other, but I just wanted to get it out.

"I'm pregnant."

Jacob stopped chewing. He stared at me in shock before swallowing down the last bite of cake hard. "Say that again?"

The second time wasn't really any easier than the first time.

"I'm pregnant," I repeated. "I'm not on birth control, so that time in the break room..."

I sat with my back stiff. I wasn't sure how he was going to react. To be honest, I wasn't really sure how I was reacting. It still felt too big and far away to really be happening.

"You're sure?" He set his fork down with a clang on the plate.

I nodded. "I took a test."

My heart stalled waiting for his response. I was going to need to see a cardiologist if this continued. Jacob either made my heart race or hold still and I was sure it wasn't good for my overall health.

A slow smile crossed his lips. He leaned back in his chair and slumped and he breathed out.

"I'm going to be a dad?"

I nodded. He wasn't freaking out, which was good.

His grin got bigger. "I'm going to be a dad!"

He jumped up and wrapped me up in his arms, swinging me around the small kitchen. Every movement spoke to joy and the breath I'd been holding in fear let out.

He wasn't upset. He was excited.

"That means an April baby." He counted on his fingers to do the math. He grinned and his eyes sparkled.

"You're not mad?" I asked, still shocked that telling him was this easy.

"Mad? Hannah, I've dreamed of having a family. I've always wanted kids." He paused and took my hands in his. "I know it's corny, but I always wanted it to be you."

"Really?"

He blushed. "You were perfect in high school. I never thought you'd go for me, but I had this fantasy that someday we'd be together," he admitted. "Whenever I thought of what my future family would look like, you were always there."

I kissed him. I kissed him with pure joy and happiness.

"We're going to be a family," I told him. "The three of us."

He grinned so wide I could barely believe his face could show that much happiness. "We're going to be a family."

# CHAPTER 27

*I*t was official. The town hated me.

To be fair, they were pretty unhappy with Jacob, but they took the majority of it out on me.

I was the "other woman." I was the reason Jacob and Katie broke up. I was the interloper who was tempting the good doctor away.

Despite the fact that none of this was true didn't matter. It was the will of the Ladies' Bridge Club. I was cast as the villain in their eyes.

It manifested in small ways. My number was never called at the deli. The checkout line somehow always "broke down" right before it was my turn to checkout. No one would speak to me on the street. I started bringing my lunch instead of going out. I drove to the next town over to buy my groceries.

Not everyone was awful. Katie's Bakery still made me the best sandwiches. Katie made sure her employees knew not to mess with me or Dr. Matthews. They honored her request because she was "being the bigger person" according to the Ladies' Bridge Club.

186

It just made her more perfect in their eyes. I didn't blame Katie, but it was rather discouraging.

It was lunch time and I was getting a grilled cheese sandwich. I'd brought a frozen meal from home, but Donna took it out of the freezer and left it on the counter to melt. She said it was an accident since she was cleaning the freezer out, but I had a hard time believing it.

So, I stood in line at Katie's Bakery. Luckily, the tourists didn't know my history and talked amicably among themselves as we waited. The locals didn't say anything, which was nice. It was nice to have a moment that didn't feel like I was universally hated.

"Don't get discouraged," Katie said, handing me my sandwich and an extra bag of chips. "They just need to get the next gossip going and they'll forget all about you."

I sighed. I knew she was right, but I had no idea how long that was going to be. And given that my pregnancy could very well be the next piece of gossip, the sentiment wasn't as uplifting as Katie hoped it would be.

"Thanks, Katie." I smiled and turned to nearly run into Karina.

"There you are!" Karina said, giving me a big hug. "Are you staying to eat?"

"I was thinking I'd go back to the office…"

"Leigh Ann and I have a table outside. There's a breeze and it's great. Come sit with us," Karina said, taking my arm. She smiled around the room, making sure that everyone knew her loyalty was with me.

God bless that girl.

Sitting outside under the large table umbrella was Leigh Ann. Her face lit up as soon as she saw me.

"Aunt Hannah!" She grinned and ran over to give me a hug. I snuggled into her, smelling the sunshine on her hair.

"I'll be right back with lunch," Karina told her daughter. She flashed me a smile and went back inside.

"Do you want to see my scar?" Leigh Ann asked. Without waiting for an answer, she lifted her bright pink tank top to show me the little scars from the surgery. They'd managed to do it all laparoscopically, so the scars were tiny and healing fast.

"Wow," I told her. "You were so brave."

She grinned. "Plus, I have a loose tooth."

"You are having one heck of a summer." I grinned at her and she grinned right back. I slipped on an over-sized pair of sunglasses that managed to hide a lot of my face. It was more for the summer sun than hiding, but they were good for both.

"Are you gonna marry Dr. Matthews?" she asked me, smoothing out the front of her shirt.

I didn't know what to say to that. We hadn't talked about it. I was pregnant, but that didn't mean that I wanted to rush into marriage. I would love to marry Jacob, but I also wanted it to be a mutual thing and for the right reasons.

"I don't know," I answered truthfully. "It's kind of complicated."

Leigh Ann nodded like she understood. "You should marry him. Then he'd be my uncle and come to all my parties. Mary Louise would be so jealous."

I chuckled. "I will make sure to tell him that."

"What are you two giggling about over here?" Karina asked, coming up to the table with sandwiches and drinks. She set a meal down in front of her daughter with a smile.

"Aunt Hannah's gonna marry Dr. Matthews," Leigh Ann explained.

Karina raised an eyebrow at me. "Is that so?"

"That's what Leigh Ann wants," I quickly told her. "She wants Mary Louise to be jealous."

Karina shook her head. "The two of them were inseparable this spring, but Mary Louise got a new bicycle and has been lording it over Leigh Ann."

I nodded. The drama of girls started young.

"So, tell me. How are things between you and Dr. Matthews?" Karina gave me a sly grin as she sipped on her soda. "You told me some things, but I want more."

I glanced over at Leigh Ann, but she was now engrossed in her sandwich.

"Things are good. Well, as good as they can be with the town telling him to break up with me and get back with Katie." I picked at my sandwich. Two bites and I was full. I knew I should eat, but it no longer looked appetizing.

"You two are perfect for one another, you know," Karina took a big bite of her tuna sandwich. The smell made my stomach flip a little and I shifted so I wouldn't be so close.

"What do you mean?"

"He's the bad boy and you were Miss Perfect," Karina explained. "Plus, I see the way he looks at you. He looks at you the way I look at pie."

I chuckled at the image in my head. Karina loved her pie.

"I heard they are opening up a new hospital across the highway," Karina said. "It shouldn't be too bad a commute. Not that I want you to go work there," she quickly explained. "Just in case the town gets to you."

I nodded. Jacob and I had already talked about it. Dr. Taggert wasn't happy with him and he had two weeks to turn things around. At least Dr. Taggert was giving him a chance. There was still a very good chance I would be fired soon, though. If enough patients refused to come because of me, I would be a liability to the clinic.

Still, we both were brushing up our resumes. I hated it. I'd just gotten comfortable here and I really liked my job. Jacob loved being a small town doctor more than Karina liked pie.

That, and with the baby coming... I hadn't told Karina that yet. I hadn't told anyone but Jacob, and I didn't dare tell her in a crowded place like this.

"Oh, Leigh Ann don't tip the cup..." Karina motioned to her daughter to stop tipping her ice laden soda up, but it was too late. "...like that."

Ice, soda, and straw all rained down on Leigh Ann's face. Her eyes went big at the sudden cold and she let out a yelp of surprise as her shirt suddenly became very cold and wet.

Karina sighed. "Let's go get you cleaned up. We'll be right back, Hannah. Don't leave, okay?"

"I'll stay, but just for you," I promised.

Karina took her daughter's hand and led her inside to the restroom to get cleaned up. I sunk down in my chair, keeping my back to the street and hoping that no one recognized me.

"Did you hear about Cassandra Reynolds?" A woman's voice said behind me. I snuck a peak to see two local women sit at the table across from us. They were both active members of the Ladies' Bridge Club and I assumed they just didn't see me sitting there.

"No," the second woman said, taking her seat. "What about her? Who is she?"

"She's Libby's daughter" the first woman explained. "She just graduated college."

"Oh, yes. I remember. Dark hair. Quiet."

"She's pregnant," the first woman announced, her voice haughty and condescending.

"No!"

"Yes. And by Richard Smoke's boy."

"You mean the little boy that used to eat dirt?" the second woman asked.

"He's grown now and manages the feed lot, but yes."

"Oh my." Second woman fanned herself and if she had pearls on I think she would have clutched them. "What in the world is the town coming to? I thought we raised our children better than this."

"It's a disgrace is what it is," the first woman replied. "How does such a thing happen?"

*Well*, I thought to myself, *when a man and a woman start feeling something and they act on it...*

It's not *that* complicated.

"Libby is all excited about a grand baby, but honestly, they aren't married. It's just not something that I, or the town, should abide." The first woman crossed her arms and preened.

I ducked as low in my seat as possible and prayed that they didn't recognize me. Listening to them was like having a running commentary on how my future was going to go. I could just hear it:

*"Did you hear about Hannah O'Leary? She pregnant. The horror!"*

It made me want to run and hide, but I'd promised Karina I'd stay and I was afraid if I moved they'd see me. I half suspected the members of the Ladies' Bridge Club to be like the T-Rex. Maybe they couldn't see me if I didn't move.

Luckily, Karina and Leigh Ann appeared. Karina looked frustrated.

"We have to go change," Karina announced. "They have paper towels, but she's soaked through."

"No worries," I told her quietly. "I was just heading back to work."

Karina gave me a hug followed by Leigh Ann. I didn't even mind that I had a wet spot on my scrub top because it was good to hug my favorite kid. Well, favorite kid outside my body.

"I'll see you guys soon," I said as we went our separate directions.

I smiled as Leigh Ann reached up and took Karina's hand

in hers as they walked across the street. I could see the small, proud smile cross Karina's face.

I was going to have that. Even if this town was awful and hated me, I was going to be a mother. They couldn't take that away from me. It wasn't the end of the world if I had to find a new job and stay on the outskirts of town.

I could make it work.

Losing the clinic would be a huge financial and emotional blow to Jacob, but I knew he could get a job at the hospital in thirty seconds of walking in the door. Our lives would change. Our hours wouldn't be quite as regular and we wouldn't get to work together like we did now, but we would make it work.

For the sake of our child, we could do it.

With a new found sense of hope, I flashed a smile at the two Ladies' Bridge Club members. They both looked aghast at me, which just made me laugh. Just wait until they heard the rest of the gossip.

*"Did you hear about Hannah O'Leary?"*

# CHAPTER 28

"We need to talk."

I winced and was really glad I wasn't facing my mother when she said it.

I took a deep breath and slowly turned to face her.

"Okay, Mom. I get off of work in about ten minutes." I checked my watch.

She looked around the empty waiting room and shrugged. "I'll just wait here." She sat down in one of the plastic chairs and crossed her legs.

At least Donna could keep her company. They were both members of the Ladies' Bridge Club. That had to count for something, right? I tried not to panic as I finished restocking the rooms and making sure that everything was set for the night.

We'd managed to have a small amount of patients today. Apparently, people liked getting healthcare in town rather than driving forty minutes and having to redo paperwork. It wasn't fast enough, though. Dr. Taggert wasn't pleased. He was more than ready to kick Jacob and I to the curb to save his beloved clinic.

It made my heart hurt, but I understood it. It was just business.

I sighed, trying not to think about it or what talking with my mother would entail. I was half afraid she already knew I was pregnant, even though I hadn't seen her since I found out. My mom always knew my secrets. I secretly suspected that it was a benefit of motherhood and I hoped that I would gain the ability with my child.

I took my time finishing stocking, but my mother knew she could outlast me. She waited patiently in the waiting room making small talk with Donna about the weather. I wasn't sure how someone could talk about rain and the possibility of rain for a straight ten minutes, but they did.

I poked my head into Jacob's office.

"My mom's here."

"As a patient?" Concern crossed his face and he subconsciously reached for his stethoscope.

"No. She wants to talk to me," I told him.

He relaxed slightly. "Good luck. You going to tell her?"

"No way in hell. I love my mom, but I don't think she's ready for that bombshell just yet."

"You're going to have to tell her eventually," he said gently. I stuck my tongue out at him and went out to the waiting room.

"Okay. What did you want to talk about?" I asked my mom, trying to sound confident and casual.

"We're going to dinner," she informed me. "So grab your things. It's my treat."

I gave her a sideways glance. "You sure you want to be seen in town with me?"

"Hannah, even if I don't agree with some of your decisions, I still love you." Her eyes were genuine and for a moment I felt like things might be okay. My mom loved me.

"Okay." I grabbed my purse and together we left the clinic.

"Where are we going?" I asked as I got into my mother's car. She waited until I was safely buckled before pulling out of the parking lot.

"The diner," she replied.

I raised an eyebrow.

"You're with me. No one will spit in your food or do anything stupid," she said, shaking her head like I was over-reacting.

Still, I was thinking of only ordering things that came deep fried and I knew exactly what they were supposed to look like.

We pulled into the diner's parking lot. It was quieter than I expected for dinner time.

"Where is everyone?" I asked, looking around. Maybe they had heard I was coming and were leaving the restaurant.

"It's poker night," my mom informed me. "They're having their big match tonight."

I nodded. That's why my father wasn't having dinner with us. He was at the poker night. I hoped he was feeling okay and knew not to drink too much. I worried about him.

All eyes turned on me when we walked in the front door. It took everything I had not to bolt, but my mom made sure to grab my arm so I couldn't get away.

"Table for two," she said clearly as we walked in. We got a little table in the corner. I liked it because I wasn't the center of attention over here.

We both looked at the menus silently, as if we didn't already have the entire thing memorized. It was a stall tactic for both of us.

"How are you, Hannah?" my mom asked softly, setting her menu down. "I worry about you."

"I'm okay, Mom." I did my best to smile.

"I'm sorry about the way things have happened. I always suspected there wasn't much chemistry between Dr. Matthews and Katie, but they were just so perfect on paper. His mother was so adamant..." She sighed. "Anyway, I wanted to apologize to you for my behavior."

I stared at my mom, tears forming in my eyes. "You didn't do anything wrong."

"Yes I did. I didn't come right out and support you. I went along with Ladies' Bridge Club because they're my friends." She reached forward and took my hands. "But, you're my daughter."

"Thank you, Mama," I whispered, not really trusting my voice.

She squeezed my hands and then went back to her menu. "I think I'll have a burger. They always have good burgers here."

That's how I knew she was serious. My mom didn't dwell on important things. She could talk about the weather for hours, but she would only say the important stuff once. We were good now. She had forgiven me for smearing the family name and sleeping with Dr. Matthews.

"I think I just want the cheese curds," I replied. It was the only thing on the menu that sounded good. When my mother frowned, I followed up with, "I had a big lunch."

"Did you hear that Cassidy Reynolds is having a baby?" My mom smiled. "Libby is so excited. It wasn't planned, but very much wanted. Apparently a doctor told her she'd never get pregnant. She's with Rich Smokes. They aren't married because they were waiting to save up the money for a big wedding. Now, they're eloping."

"Really?" My heart lightened hearing the other side of the story. "That's actually a really happy story."

"I know, right?" My mom leaned forward. "It's all drama

in the society about it, though. Libby's so happy, but that means she's going to have a grandchild before Rachel, and Rachel isn't happy about that. Her daughter's been married for three years and no babies yet."

I was about to say something when the front door of the diner burst open and a gaggle of men poured through it.

"I won!" my dad shouted, waving his hat around as he came in. "I won the tournament!"

"Oh, there will be no living with him now," my mother whispered, shaking her head.

I chuckled and smiled as my dad went up to the bar and ordered a round of drinks for his friends. He pulled out a thick stack of bills and slammed a hundred dollar bill down on the counter.

"How much money was the tournament worth?" I asked, eyeing the wad of cash in my dad's hand.

"Each member had to put in fifty dollars," my mom answered. "There were some re-buys, but you know your dad never goes for that."

Given that nearly every adult male that could get away from their kids or work was part of the poker group, that meant a lot of money. I was rather proud of my dad. It was definitely something that made him happy.

The diner got much louder with the men buying drinks and praising my dad for his poker skills. I recognized many faces. There was my dad, Dr. Taggert, the minister, Mr. Abrams who owned the grocery store, and several other of my father's friends. At one point my dad came over to our table. He kissed my mother on the lips, making her blush.

"Can you believe I won?" he asked us, his eyes dancing with delight. "I've never won before."

"What was your secret this time, Dad?" I asked him.

He glanced around and then leaned forward so the poker group couldn't hear him. "I'm not drunk. I've only had water and root beer all night. I can read their bluffs like a book."

He pointed to the dark bubbly glass of liquid next to him. I had thought he was drinking a dark stout like he usually did, but I smelled it to find it really was just root-beer.

"I should have thought of this years ago," he admitted. "Dinner's on me, girls."

He grinned, picked up his drink, and went back to hanging with his buddies.

I knew he would be exhausted later. I could already see the dark circles under his eyes and he leaned heavy against the bar. This would drain his energy, but it made him so happy I didn't have the heart to tell him to stop. These were the memories I wanted to have of him.

Many of the poker club members gave me dirty looks. Despite the restaurant being crowded, my mother and I had plenty of room around our table. However, my water was knocked over three times and somehow my lemonade never made it out.

I tried to ignore them. My father was happy and my mother didn't hate me. I didn't really care what the rest of the town thought. They could keep on giving me dirty looks and bumping the waitress with my drink so it would spill.

"Just go home," one man said, walking past me. "You're not wanted here."

My mother gave him a death glare, but he was already gone.

"Have people really been treating you like this?" Mom asked, looking around.

"Yeah." I played with my food for a moment. "I'm actually thinking of applying at the hospital for a job. It's a commute, but people don't want me in town anymore."

My mother frowned, but she didn't disagree with me.

"Bob? Bob, are you okay?" I heard my dad ask over the

sound of the TV and conversations. There was something about his voice that made my internal alarms go off.

I looked over to see my dad standing next to Dr. Bob Taggert at the bar. Dr. Taggert was slumped over his drink and my dad was shaking his shoulder. Something about it made my skin crawl. My dad shook his friend's shoulder and Dr. Taggert groaned.

Something was definitely wrong.

"Hannah!" my dad shouted, followed by a heavy cough.

At this point, the fellow restaurant patrons went quiet. It might have been my name or the terror in my dad's voice, but suddenly all eyes were on me and my dad.

I hurried over to the bar. Dr. Taggert's skin was clammy and white. His eyes were glazed over and he had his right arm clutched to his chest.

"Dr. Taggert? Are you okay?" I asked, putting my hand on his left wrist.

He didn't answer me with more than a shake of his head. His pulse under my fingertips was thready and erratic.

The first thought through my head: Oh shit.

Then, my training took over.

"Dad, I need you to call 911. Mr. Abrams, I need you to call Dr. Matthews and tell him that Dr. Taggert is having a heart attack at the diner. He'll get here before the ambulance will." I looked up long enough to make sure my dad nodded at me. I pointed to one of the younger men. "Help me get him on the floor. If he falls, he'll hurt himself. Everyone else, we need some space and a clear path to the door. Mr. Canes, please make sure that happens."

I made sure to look at them and make sure everyone had a set job so that things would actually get done. I'd done several full Code Blues at the hospital and even there it was important to assign roles so nothing got forgotten and no one thought someone else would do it.

The room went silent as two men helped me get Dr. Taggert on the floor. I kept checking his pulse and making sure that he was breathing. His breaths were shallow, but there. His pulse wasn't much better.

I really didn't want to do CPR today. This was not how I had envisioned my evening going.

"Aspirin. I need an aspirin. Who has one?" I asked, looking around the room.

"I got one," a voice said from the back. The owner of the grocery store came forward and handed me a bottle of pills.

"Thanks," I told him, wrenching the bottle open and grabbing one of the tablets. I put it in Dr. Taggert's mouth and he thankfully started to chew it. He gave me a small nod as he swallowed down the medication. I was glad he was still conscious enough to help out.

"911 wants to talk to you," my dad announced. He looked pale and like he might pass out at any moment, which I certainly didn't need.

"Okay. Give me the phone and go sit with mom," I told him. I set his phone on speaker and put it on the floor beside me. "This is Hannah O'Leary. I'm a nurse here. I've given him one tablet of adult aspirin, which he has chewed and swallowed. Dr. Matthews is on his way."

I was in full nurse mode now. It was science, medicine, and muscle memory. There was no fear, or nerves. I knew there would be if I stopped, so I didn't. I just kept doing assessment after assessment and reporting everything to the 911 operator.

I've done CPR twice in my life. I didn't want this to be the third. CPR is hard and doing it on someone you know is brutal.

"I'm here," Dr. Matthews announced, running through the doors. He had his big black medical bag as well as an AED with him. If I hadn't been in work mode, I would have kissed him.

I rattled off Dr. Taggert's stats as we placed the AED and turned it on. No shock was advised, so Dr. Matthews handed me an IV kit to get started. I felt a lot better knowing there was a computer watching Dr. Taggert's heart instead of me just feeling and hoping for a pulse.

I had the IV placed when the shriek of the ambulance broke through my thoughts.

The paramedics had Dr. Taggert in the gurney and into the ambulance in two breaths. Everything blurred now that someone else was in charge. I did remember one of the paramedics telling me I did a great job on the IV, though.

Dr. Matthews went with the paramedics to the hospital. The energy and clarity of what I was doing vanished with them out the door. I stood in the center of the entrance to the diner, panting as the ambulance roared off with a shriek and a flurry of lights. I still had my gloves on from starting the IV.

The room was silent for a moment.

"Good job, Hannah," my mother said, coming and giving me a hug. She took my arm and led me back to the table where my father sat.

I collapsed into a seat, suddenly very tired. Someone put a beer in front of me, but I pushed it away. Instead I stole a sip of my dad's root-beer, grateful for the sugar.

"He said he just had indigestion," my dad said, sipping at his root-beer. He took another deep sip, trying to wrap his head around what just happened. "I'm glad you were able to help, Hannah."

I smiled at my dad. "Me, too, Dad."

"Good job, Hannah," a man said walking past my table. Then another. Someone patted my shoulder and thanked me. Another walked past and said I did good.

"It was a good thing you were here," my mother said after a moment, loud enough for those standing close to hear. "Imagine if she had just gone home tonight. Or left early. Or worked somewhere else."

Some of those standing close managed to look bashful.

Now that everything was over, I just wanted to curl up in bed and sleep for the next eighteen hours.

"You should get Dad home," I told mom. He was pale now and shaky. The excitement of his poker win had worn off and now he looked pale and tired. He'd already overdone things for the day, and witnessing a heart attack had put him over into exhausted.

"Can you get home okay?" Mom asked.

"If you can drop me off at the clinic, I'll be fine," I told her. I didn't plan on driving just yet. My hands were still shaking. I was just going to sit in my car and freak out for a minute.

We stood up and made our way to the door. The other patrons called out their good nights to my parents, and a few of them even to me.

Outside the night air was humid but relaxing. It was warm, but not hot out. The stars twinkled over head and the cicadas hummed in the trees. I took a deep breath in of the sweet air and sighed.

We piled into the car and took the short drive back to the clinic. We left Dad's truck and Dr. Mathew's motorcycle in the parking lot. I hoped things were going well.

Mom pulled into the parking lot of the clinic just as Dr. Matthews texted me an update. Dr. Taggert was stable. He was in the Cardiac ICU and scheduled for a round of tests in the morning. They suspected he'd be having surgery sometime tomorrow.

I let out a long sigh of relief and let my parents know. My dad's shoulders relaxed with the news and he smiled.

"You did good tonight, Kiddo," he told me. "I'm proud of you."

"Me too," my mom chimed in.

I nearly burst into tears.

Instead I just thanked them, gave them each hugs, reminded my dad to take his medicine and get some rest, and then sat in my car.

As soon as I was alone, I cried and laughed and then fell asleep in the parking lot.

# CHAPTER 29

We had ten patients in the clinic the next day, as well as new future appointments to make up lost appointments. Mr. Abrams was coming in. So was the preacher and his wife. The next day we almost had a full schedule. By the end of the week, we were just a few appointments shy of a regular day.

Things were slowly getting back to normal.

Still, I secretly hoped that Abigail St. James would continue to see the doctor in the next town over, even if I was fired. The further that woman was from me, even in my head, the better. It was petty, but I didn't care.

Friday came with the news that Dr. Taggert was on his way home from the hospital. He was still weak and recovering from surgery, but healing faster than expected. He was banned from working at the clinic until he was one-hundred percent, but I had a feeling that he'd somehow sneak in to see patients by the end of next week.

As for me, I kept busy. With our schedule back to having patients, I found myself worrying less about losing my job.

We were keeping the clinic up and running, which meant that Jacob's contract with Dr. Taggert was safe.

At least for now.

I liked being busy. It kept my mind from thinking about anything from work. I luckily hadn't had much morning sickness yet, but I kept a two liter of ginger ale out in my car just in case. I was still too early to use the office ultrasound or Doppler machine, but I walked wistfully past those rooms more than I needed to.

I still hadn't told anyone but Jacob about the pregnancy.

To be honest, I was too scared to. I had heard the rumors about Cassandra. My mother's version was so much kinder than the rumors I'd heard around town. Living in a small town, the only interesting thing that we could count on was gossip. And because humans love to gossip, things became a game of telephone that skewed all the information.

Last I heard at the supermarket, Cassandra was carrying twins from her secret lover in Kentucky and the grandparents were going to sue for adoption. Cassandra was apparently moving to Alaska and becoming a lesbian because of the stress.

None of that was true, but it was being repeated around town. Every whisper had it's own version of what the unwed mother was going to do.

Cassandra's mother had lost business to her store and Cassandra hadn't shown her face in town since the rumor broke. I didn't blame her. I knew exactly how that felt. I knew how it felt to enter the grocery store and suddenly have everyone watching exactly what you bought. I knew how it felt to have random people come up and ask inappropriate questions about my personal life.

I knew.

And I knew it was going to happen to me again.

I waved goodbye to a patient and went to clean and prep

the room. I paused, putting a hand to my stomach. There was life there. There was someone amazing growing inside of me. I was going to shelter this baby from the worst of the world, even if it meant taking the rumors on myself.

I sighed. I could already hear the rumors that would spread about me. Despite the fact that it wasn't true, much of the town still blamed me for Jacob breaking up with Katie. I still heard the older women whisper "hussy" when I passed.

I could only imagine the gossip that would come about when they found out I was pregnant. Dr. Taggert had come close to firing Jacob and me. What would happen when he found out about the pregnancy?

Not only would I lose what little dignity in town I had left, but I lose my job too?

I closed my eyes and leaned against the exam table, suddenly very tired. I'd found that being pregnant took a lot of energy. I didn't know how something the size of a small bean could sap the energy from my body so quickly.

"Hey, beautiful," Jacob said, stepping inside the exam room. The door shut quietly behind him. I looked at it, almost wanting to tell him to open it. I didn't need more rumors.

"Hi," I greeted him. He kissed me gently and then opened the door back up. He was aware of what was being said and was looking out for me. "What's up?"

"I was hoping you'd come to lunch with me," he said. His smile was slightly nervous, but it was probably because the two of us going to lunch in public was socially dangerous.

"You sure?" I asked, feeling my eyebrows come together. "I don't know if the town is ready yet."

"This will help stop the rumors," he replied. I wasn't sure how that was going to happen, but he put on the puppy-dog eyes. "Please?"

"Those eyes don't work on me," I told him, turning away and crossing my arms.

"They work on everyone," he assured me, chasing me so he could stand in front of me. He made sure I could see him and he made his eyes somehow bigger.

"Nope." But my nerve was weakening. Those eyes. I could see how he managed to stay out of trouble when he was younger. Those eyes were potent.

He glanced out the door to make sure no one was in the hall before bringing his lips to my ear. His breath tickled the small hairs on my neck and made my stomach do twitter-pated somersaults.

"Come to lunch," he whispered. "I'll make it worth your while."

My knees quivered as he nibbled on my ear. I was toast. There was no way I could say no now.

"Fine," I said, trying to sound strong but instead sounding breathless.

He gave me one more kiss on the cheek before pulling away. He grinned and gave me a wink before sauntering out of the exam room with cocky confidence.

I checked my watch. I'd managed to resist him for a thirty seconds. I was getting better at it. Maybe in ten years I'd make it a whole five minutes.

I kept working until lunch time. We had a nice steady stream of patients, and for the first time in weeks, everyone managed to stay polite. No one mentioned Katie.

I almost had to think that something else was going on, but I didn't know what. Maybe saving Dr. Taggert from a heart attack was enough to turn the tide a little bit. Maybe, just maybe, the town was starting to see me as something other than a man-stealing trollop. Maybe, they now saw me as a man-stealing trollop who knows CPR.

CPR knowing people are good people to have around.

"Lunch time," Donna called from the front desk. She sounded unusually chipper. She poked her head into my office where I was charting and smiled at me. "You ready for lunch?"

I shrugged. Instead of morning sickness, I just wasn't hungry. It took effort to convince me to eat anything, and even when I did eat, I had to really focus on finishing my food. I supposed no appetite was better than nausea, though.

Donna fluttered around my doorway as I turned off my computer screen and grabbed my purse.

"Are you coming to lunch with us?" I asked her, unsure of her behavior. Ever since Dr. Taggert's heart attack, she'd been nicer, but not this nice. It was making me nervous.

"Oh, I'm eating in town, but not with you," she quickly replied. She looked me over, sighed with a soft smile, and then left.

I stood there, unsure of what to do with that. Whatever it was, I was just glad she wasn't pulling my lunches from the freezer anymore. I liked happy Donna much better than angry Donna.

I shook my head and headed out to the lobby. Jacob stood by the front desk, playing with a pen. He wore dark gray dress slacks with a cream button-up shirt. It was a little dressy for work, but if he had a meeting at the hospital later it would make sense.

"You ready?" he asked, a smile crossing his face as he saw me.

"Yeah," I replied. From across the lobby, I heard Donna sigh happily. "Where are we going?"

"It's a surprise," he told me. He reached for my hand. He was sweating even though the air conditioning was running like crazy.

We took the short walk from the clinic to the center of town. The humidity was high, but the day was cool and slightly cloudy. It was a wonderful day to be outside, and it seemed like everyone was out today. I waved to Karina and Leigh Ann as we walked past them in a shop. I even thought I saw my mom and dad in town.

Jacob bounced with energy. I figured the meeting he was dressed for must be important if he was this keyed up. He walked faster than usual and then would slow down as he realized he was dragging me along. But, then he'd just end up walking fast again.

"Are you okay?" I asked him after he slowed down for the third time. "You seem a little anxious."

He let out a nervous laugh. "Just hungry, I guess."

"Okay…" I shook my head, but followed him to the town square.

In the very center of downtown Riversville is a small park. It has a cute little gazebo and a water feature that looks like a waterfall turning into a small stream. Some bronze statues of children and birds play endlessly in the looping water. There's a nice open space full of green grass with trees on the edges. The Fourth of July city picnic was always held here and in May and June the gazebo often held weddings.

Today it seemed like half the town was picnicking on the grass. I wondered if there was a community event today that I didn't know about. It would explain why Jacob wanted to come have lunch.

Jacob sped up as we approached the gazebo. Strangely, the space under the gazebo was empty. Usually, it was considered one of the prime spots since it was in the shade, but today everyone had chosen to be on the grass.

There were three small steps up to the gazebo and Jacob paused before the first one and took a deep breath. He looked over at me and smiled.

"You know I love you, right?" he asked me.

"Of course I do," I replied. Something was up. I wasn't

sure what, but something was going to happen. "What do you have planned?"

He flashed me a grin and then looked at my stomach before coming back up to my eyes. "Something good. I hope."

I frowned in confusion, but he just started up the stairs. I followed.

Jacob stood in the center of the gazebo, his hands in his pockets with the thumbs hanging out. He looked confident other than the nervous smile and the fact that he was tapping his heel.

"Seriously, what's going on?" I asked, joining him in the gazebo.

"Hannah Louise O'Leary, I love you," he announced. He spoke loud and clearly and the crowd around the gazebo went quiet. All eyes were on the two of us. Everyone in town was watching what happened next.

If this was Jacob's plan for the town to see us as a couple, he had certainly found a dramatic way to do so.

"I've loved you since that first lesson in biology class," he continued. He reached forward and took my hands in his. His normally surgeon steady hands were shaking. "You've been my dream girl for as long as I can remember. To find you again, was luck. To have you love me back was something I had only imagined could be possible."

He looked into my eyes. Suddenly, I didn't care about the crowd. I didn't care that the entire town was watching us. With him looking at me like that, we were the only two people in the world. The gazebo was our universe.

Slowly, he knelt before me and reached into his back pocket. My breath caught and my brain went fuzzy for a moment. Suddenly, everything from the way he was dressed to the entire town being at the park, made sense.

"Hannah Louise O'Leary, I love you more than anything." His voice cracked slightly as he opened a small black velvet box. "Would you make me the happiest man in the world and be my wife?"

A diamond ring glittered in the box, but I didn't care about the ring. It could have been a piece of string for all I cared. It wasn't the ring that was important, it was the question.

"Yes," I whispered, emotion catching in my throat. "Yes, please!"

The most beautiful smile lit up his face as he rose and kissed me. I kissed him back with a joy so intense I could barely breathe. He wanted to spend forever with me. I wanted to spend eternity with him.

A cheer rose up behind us and I remembered that we weren't alone. Jacob held onto me as we broke the kiss and glanced around.

My parents were there, cheering. Karina and Leigh Ann cheered and Leigh Ann even had a noise maker to help her. I found Jacob's parents and saw that his father was cheering and his mother at least looked moderately pleased.

"Congratulations, you two!" Katie said, coming up the steps of the gazebo. She had a huge smile on her face as she hugged me.

"Thanks," I said, feeling a blush hit my face.

She grinned and then faced the crowd. "There's engagement cake on the north end of the lawn," she announced. "Make sure to congratulate the new couple!"

She gave us both a quick hug before hurrying off to the north end. I now noticed a table with something on it. Katie's assistant lifted a box and revealed a beautiful cake. On the top were two figures, one wearing a white doctor's coat and the other nursing scrubs.

All around us, the town clapped and cheered as he slid the ring onto my finger. It was simple, but I thought it was the most beautiful ring in the entire world.

"Kiss her again!" someone called out.

So he did.

I was laughing and crying. My mother ran over and gave me a big hug, followed by my father.

"Did you two know about this?" I asked them.

"Well, he did come over and ask permission earlier this week," my dad replied. "Brought me a nice bottle of scotch and a breathing treatment."

My jaw dropped open just a little.

"Don't worry, I'm saving the scotch for something important," Dad said, giving me another hug. He was much stronger today, and I was so grateful.

"He brought me flowers and chocolate," my mom informed me. She grinned. "I think I'm warming up to the idea of him being around all the time."

Jacob laughed, keeping his arm wrapped around my waist. He wasn't letting me go.

"Congratulations," his mother said coming up behind my parents.

I swallowed hard, not quite sure of how this was going to go.

"Thank you, Mrs. Matthews." My hand tightened on Jacob's.

"Jacob won't stop singing your praises," Mrs. Matthews continued. "To be honest, I've never seen him so happy." She smiled at her son. "And if he's happy, then I'm happy."

I let out a breath I didn't realize I was holding in. I had been afraid she'd still be gunning for him to marry Katie, despite the fact that she'd made us a beautiful cake celebrating our engagement.

"Congratulations," Officer Matthews said, giving me a gentle hug. "Welcome to the family. At least you know the crazy you're getting in to.

I chuckled and he laughed. Karina waved from across the

lawn. Leigh Ann already had a massive piece of cake and frosting all over her face. I waved back.

"Is this real?" I asked Jacob, glancing around.

He kissed my head and held me to him. "I sure hope so. This actually took a surprising amount of work."

I looked up at him. "It was wonderful."

He grinned. "Worth it, then."

"Any idea when the wedding will be?" Mrs. Matthews asked. Somehow she had a piece of cake in her hands. Probably one of her aides had gotten it for her.

"Soon," Jacob replied. "I don't want to wait. I've waited since high school."

"I don't want anything big," I said. "Just family. Friends."

"I already claim making the cake," Katie announced bringing Jacob and I a slice of cake each. "Just so you know."

I took a bite and moaned softly. It was vanilla, but rich and creamy and somehow more vibrant than regular cake. Maybe it was the occasion, or maybe it was Katie's abilities. Either way, it was amazing.

"Done," I told her, quickly taking another.

"The courthouse is open for a few more hours," Mrs. Matthews observed, licking the last of her frosting from her fork.

My eyes widened in surprise. I was glad she was onboard with the wedding, but offering it up for today?

"What? I want grand babies," she said with a shrug. My mother laughed.

"What about it?" Jacob asked, turning to me. "Want to head to the courthouse?"

"Seriously?"

Jacob nodded. "If you want some time..."

"No. Let's do. I just want to wear a dress." I pointed down to my work scrubs. "I'm not exactly dressed at the moment."

"I have something you can wear," my mother said, stepping forward. "It's at home, but it will fit you."

"Okay. I'll meet you at the courthouse in thirty minutes then?"

Jacob grinned and kissed me.

"Does it count that you've now seen me on the day of our wedding?" I asked when he released me.

Our parents both laughed. "I think it'll be okay," my father assured me.

Jacob met my gaze one last time before my mother pulled me away. My fingers slid out from his, easily, but not willingly. I didn't want to leave him, even though I knew we'd be together in just a little bit.

# CHAPTER 30

*I* had dreamed of marrying Jacob Matthews since the first day he said two words to me. I'd always imagined a dress and a church, but to be honest, I didn't care how I married him. Just that I married him.

Today, I stood outside the town courthouse in a long white lace dress.

I wore my mother's wedding dress. She'd kept it all these years with the hope that I would one day wear it. It was long and in a bohemian style from the late seventies, but simple enough that it was eternally classic.

I loved it. I loved that it was a piece of my parents' marriage and that it would now be a part of mine.

Karina brought me flowers from her garden. I had sunflowers and daisies, mixed with beautiful orange lilies. I couldn't have picked out more beautiful flowers from a florist if I had tried.

Katie had called and told me she was taking care of the cake. And the food. Mrs. Matthews said the gazebo was ours for the rest of the day. Someone called their band, and another person started bringing chairs.

We were having a reception in the park and the entire town was invited after the wedding.

Now, I stood outside the courthouse with my parents. It was quiet other than the sound of cicadas and birds. The sun cast a warm orange glow that made the world feel brighter and more magical than usual.

I swallowed hard as my dad took one arm and my mother the other. Together, they walked me into the courthouse.

The judge waited for us in the main courtroom. The room was usually for the small court cases and minor legal issues of the city and county. It appeared that the entire town was sitting in the benches and chairs packed into the room. Everyone was happy and smiling.

Jacob turned, as did the entire courtroom, as I walked in.

I saw only Jacob. The rest of the town faded from my mind.

Jacob filled my world. He was all I saw. He had put on his suit jacket and a tie, and someone had gotten him a daisy boutonniere to match my bouquet. He smiled and I knew I was making the right decision. I could feel it in my bones. Every inch of me new that I was supposed to do this with him.

He was my match. We'd always been meant to be.

This was fate. It was how things were supposed to be.

And so, we got married an hour after he proposed.

We told everyone that Francine came early.

One of the perks of being married to the town doctor is that no one questions him when he says medical things. As far as the town knew, Francine was just an amazingly big preemie.

Francine Grace Matthews was born at two thirty in the morning on April second. Jacob delivered her himself. We were thankfully at the hospital, and one of the other doctors took over for him once the baby arrived so that he could be a parent and husband rather than a doctor.

She was the most beautiful thing I'd ever seen in my life. It made waiting to meet her worth it. Even her cries were beautiful to me. Her tiny toes, her rosebud lips, and big blue eyes that looked just like Jacob's.

She made my heart break with too much love. I couldn't hold it all in when she was around. Even though I was exhausted, I didn't want to sleep because I just wanted to hold her and drink her perfection in.

If I thought I loved my daughter, my father absolute adored her.

For the first few weeks of her life, I shared her with him. The two of them would sit in his easy chair watching Sesame Street. He breathlessly read her the words on the screen, teaching her letters and numbers even while she slept.

I didn't know how long the two of them would have together, but I knew that my father loved his granddaughter. I was so incredibly happy that the two of them were able to meet, let alone have any time together. The cancer was winning the battle over his body, but his heart and mind belonged entirely to Francine.

Dr. Taggert signed over the clinic to Jacob while I was still pregnant. My mother was asking me to go back to work as soon as possible so that she can babysit. One of the benefits of being in a small town is that she can come to me for feedings.

Life is good.

I found love. I found my daughter. I had given up hope that my father would ever get to see me in a wedding dress, let alone meet any of his grandchildren.

Yet, he did.


Life is good.

Hey there! I'm so happy you enjoyed this book about the doctor and the nurse. There are two other books of mine coming out this month, and I'd like to share a little from each of them with you. Read on!

# THE BILLIONAIRE'S BABY ARRANGEMENT

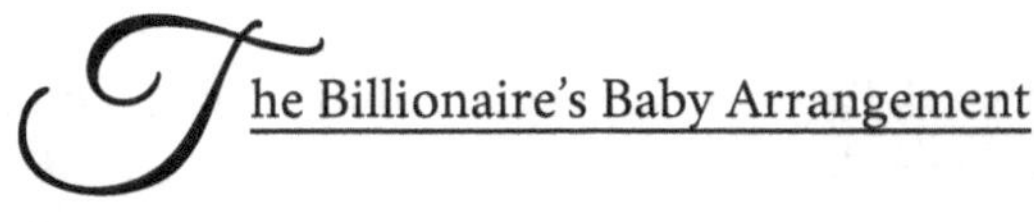

From New York Times bestselling author Krista Lakes comes a sexy standalone novel about a billionaire and the indecent proposal he gives the local barista.

Billionaire CEO Jackson Weathers needs a family for a PR boost, and I've signed a contract agreeing to give him one. A doting girlfriend in public. A wedding ceremony to invite all the socialites to. And finally, a baby for him to parade around, to show he's really a wholesome, down-to-Earth man.

I've tried to remain cynical about it. He's going to make all my dreams come true. So what if it's supposed to be a loveless marriage?

Only, his tenderness in private has me hooked. The way he kisses me drives me wild. When we make love, I lose myself to him. His body feels like it was meant to be on top of mine, like we fit together like two puzzle pieces. I can't help but begin to fall for him.

I can't tell him, or I risk losing everything. And nobody else can find out about our little "arrangement" or it will destroy his reputation. Still, I feel like I have to know how he feels, before the marriage, before the baby, before I give my entire life over to him.

Is it still just pretend?

"I was wondering when you were going to get home." Her hand went to the silky collar of her robe and she tugged on it gently to reveal just a hint of smooth skin underneath. She liked that he swallowed hard and stared.

"Work went long," he said, his eyes still glued to the bare skin of her chest. She let the robe open just a little more. "If I had known this was waiting for me, I would have been home hours ago."

She grinned and stood from the couch. She flipped off the light, letting just the pale glow from the city lights fill the room. With a grin, she undid the ties to the robe and let the fabric slide to the floor. The pale silk pooled around her ankles as she stood naked before him in the pale twilight. She knew the lack of light would hide her flaws.

His reaction made all the waiting worth it. His eyes dilated, his mouth opened, and she could see the growing bulge in his pants. She rather liked having this effect on him. She knew that he found her beautiful. She knew that he found her sexually attractive, but to see his actual reaction would never get old.

She felt like a goddess when he looked at her like that.

He reached out a finger and caressed the arch of her

collarbone, his finger then tracing the curve of her shoulder down her arm. Goosebumps popped out along her skin, but it wasn't from cold. It was pure desire at being touched. His fingers caught the swell of her breast, skimming along the curve and barely touching her.

Her nipples hardened in front of his eyes. Hunger blossomed on his face as he cupped her breast in his warm hand, his thumb rubbing against the hard nipple. Jackson's pupils nearly took over the green of his eyes.

She took a step forward, threading her hand over his shoulder and into his hair as she pressed her naked body against his suit. She could feel the warm, hard spot at her groin as she leaned in, drawing his lips to hers.

He tasted so good. Every time he kissed her he tasted better. His mouth opened and his tongue quested into her waiting mouth, tangling with her tongue. His hand was still on her breast, playing with the nipple while the other hand went to her hip and pulled her further into him.

She pulled back, gazing up at him through long lashes and grinning. She rocked her naked hips into his, feeling him harden further. With the hand not around his neck, she grabbed his tie, fisting the silk, and pulled him in for another kiss.

This kiss was urgent. She wanted to feel him inside of her. She wanted his hard length to fill her. Heat was building in her core and he was the only one who could put it out.

He kissed her, letting her be in control for a moment. She smiled as she kissed him, enjoying the idea that the naked woman was the one in control of the clothed, powerful businessman.

He groaned, and his hand tightened on her hip. She wasn't in quite as much control as he let her think. He was bigger and stronger. His hip thrust into her, letting her know that he was going to fuck her the moment he had the chance.

And she was very okay with that.
<u>The Billionaire's Baby Arrangement</u>

# CRIME BOSS BABY

rime Boss Baby

From New York Times bestselling author Krista Lakes, comes a sensual, standalone mafia romance that will have you turning the pages at record speed.

I am a mafia princess.

My family is making me marry a rival crime boss.

At first, I go along with it because it's important to my family. But then I meet *him*.

Dante is dangerous and sexy as sin. I want him physically and mentally. His talented fingers and mouth have me panting for more before he even knows my real name.

But there are parts of my past that can ruin everything. My mother's murderer is catching up to me. If he finds me, he could ruin everything. Not only that, not everyone in Dante's family is as excited about the wedding as they appear.

And then, there's news that both overjoys and terrifies me. I'm pregnant.

Can Dante save me and give me the future we both desire? Or will my past destroy everything and everyone that I care about?

# ABOUT THE AUTHOR

New York Times and USA Today Bestseller Krista Lakes is a thirtysomething who recently rediscovered her passion for writing. She is living happily ever after with her Prince Charming. Her first kid just started preschool and she is happy to welcome her second child into her life, continuing her "Happily Ever After"!

Thank you for supporting an indie author. Anything you can do, whether it be writing a review, or even simply telling a fellow reader that you enjoyed this, helps me out immensely. Thanks!

Krista would love to hear from you! Please contact her at Krista.Lakes@gmail.com or friend her on Facebook!

Further reading:

*Bad Boys and Babies*
Family Doctor's Baby
The Billionaire's Baby Arrangement
Crime Boss Baby

*Kinds of Love*
A Forever Kind of Love
A Wonderful Kind of Love

An Endless Kind of Love

*Billionaires and Brides*
Yours Completely: A Cinderella Love Story
Yours Truly: A Cinderella Love Story
Yours Royally: A Cinderella Love Story

*The "Kisses" series*
Saltwater Kisses: A Billionaire Love Story
Kisses From Jack: The Other Side of Saltwater Kisses
Rainwater Kisses: A Billionaire Love Story
Champagne Kisses: A Timeless Love Story
Freshwater Kisses: A Billionaire Love Story
Sandcastle Kisses: A Billionaire Love Story
Hurricane Kisses: A Billionaire Love Story
Barefoot Kisses: A Billionaire Love Story
Sunrise Kisses: A Billionaire Love Story
Waterfall Kisses: A Billionaire Love Story
Island Kisses: A Billionaire Love Story

*Other Novels*
I Choose You: A Secret Billionaire Romance
His Every Desire: A Billionaire Seduction
Wolf Six's Salvation: A Shifter Love Story
Burned: A New Adult Love Story
Walking on Sunshine: A Sweet Summer Romance
An American Cinderella: A Royal Love Story
Mr. Darcy's Kiss: A Contemporary Pride and Prejudice